a tale of the i·ching

HOW THE BOOK OF CHANGES BEGAN

a tale of the i·ching

How the Book of Changes Began

NEW REVISED EDITION

BY WU WEI

wisdom tree

First published in USA by Power Press
Published in 2008 by

wisdom
tree

Wisdom tree
4779/23, Ansari Road, Darya Ganj, New Delhi-110002
Ph.: 23247966/67/68

ISBN 978-81-8328-123-2

Printed at Print Perfect, New Delhi-110064

Cover design: Roger Gefvert
Interior design and production: Robert S. Tinnon Design
All interior art by Wu Wei

The symbol on the title page is the Chinese word picture for change. It was painted with five quick slashes of Wu Wei's ink brush.

For Pax

Contents

Preface

When writing appeared in China about 3000 BC, the I Ching (yee jing) was already old, having been handed down orally from generation to generation for perhaps a thousand years or more. The story of the creation of the I Ching is lost to us. All that has come down to us across the intervening fifty or sixty centuries is a name: Fu Hsi (foo shee), the man to whom the creation of the I Ching is attributed, along with the eight figures of three lines each and the sixty-four figures of six lines each which he created. Therefore, any tale that purports to relate the story of the beginning of the I Ching must be built out of imagination and insight rather than documentation.

Whenever I begin what, for me, are major projects, such as the building of a stone fireplace or the carving of a tub out of the stump of a great tree, I have found that the project takes on a life of its own and begins to develop along lines quite apart from the ones that I originally intended. Over the years I have learned to allow myself to be influenced by how the work wants to develop, and, in so doing, I become the guided rather than the guide. Therefore, I was not too surprised when that very thing happened as soon as I began to write this tale.

The original title of the book was *I Ching Divination*, and it was not to be a story but a textbook describing the I Ching and how to use it. Accordingly, the first sentence I wrote was, "There are 64 hexagrams, each one representing a particular condition or situation." Since beginnings are of critical importance, I sat back after writing that first sentence and looked at it. Yes, that was exactly how I wanted the book to begin; factually, and in a straightforward manner. But as I sat forward to write again, a new thought formed in my mind, almost as if it had come of its own volition, and I wrote, "It had been a wonderful harvest, as bountiful as any farmer could desire. Five years in a row had Heaven smiled upon them and blessed their labors, and now, in this sixth year, the harvest was greater than ever before." The words came so smoothly and effortlessly that it made me smile. "So," I thought, "it's to be *that* kind of a story."

I am a sentimental person, and there are several places in the story that, as I wrote them, tears came to my eyes. Even to this day I cannot read those parts of the story without my tears appearing. Perhaps it is true that we live many lifetimes, carrying forward the work we began in earlier lifetimes during later lifetimes. I am not suggesting that in an earlier life I was such a grand and singular person as Fu Hsi, but perhaps I played some minor role that permitted me to observe a bit of that time period, and memories of that life still lie in some remote part of my gene pool, tugging at my heartstrings when I write about the beginning of the I Ching.

Whatever this story may be, fact, fiction, fantasy, or combination, I humbly offer it to you in the hope that some of my love for the I Ching and its great wisdom carries through to you, that you find enjoyment in reading this tale of the I Ching, and that your understanding and appreciation of the great book is expanded.

I want to thank Roger Gefvert for his enlightened cover design, which set the standard for the beauty of the book and reflects so well the look and feel of the timeless quality of the I Ching itself.

And I want to thank Robert Tinnon for his inspired interior design and layout, which correspond so well to the cover and to the clarity and spirituality of the I Ching.

Wu Wei

AUTHOR'S APOLOGY

I humbly apologize to the great master, Fu Hsi, to whom belongs all credit for the conception and formation of the I Ching, for presuming to be able to write the tale of the beginning of the I Ching. That I have done so is only because of my love of the great book and that I hope in my small way to share the great gift of divine guidance with the people of the world. Please accept my minor labors in that spirit.

Your servant,

Wu Wei

AUTHOR'S APOLOGY TO ALL READERS

I humbly apologize to you for my presumption that I know something that you do not and for my egotistical assumption that I know anything at all. All information comes from one source, the Universe, and since we are all part of it, its information belongs to us all and is available to each of us. On the small chance that I have spent more time seeking out information about the I Ching and ways to use it than you have, and therefore may have received information which you may not have yet received, and because I want you to have as much information as possible about the I Ching, I risk this great presumption. Please overlook and forgive my immodesty. That I undertake this work at all is only because of my love for the great wisdom and my sincere desire to impart it to you.

Your humble and insignificant servant,

Wu Wei

CHAPTER ONE

The Harvest

It had been a wonderful harvest, as bountiful as any farmer could desire. Five years in a row had Heaven smiled upon them and blessed their labors, and now, in this sixth year, the harvest was greater than ever before. What cause for rejoicing there was, what happiness could be seen upon every face. All concerns had been flung to the winds, and there was dancing in the streets.

Yet among the villagers there was one who was concerned. Tan—the dreamer; the young man who was forever shirking his chores and who could usually be found in the forests or the fields, wandering aimlessly, his thoughts far away from his assigned tasks—he was concerned. "And why shouldn't I be concerned?" he said to himself? "Did not our great sage, Fu Hsi, tell us that after all fullness comes emptiness? That after all increase comes decrease? And worse, the greater the increase, the greater the decrease? Did not Fu Hsi tell us that it is only possible to fall from a great height after one has ascended to that height?" And Tan was filled with foreboding.

At the gathering of the elders one particular evening, he appeared and asked to speak. Surprise showed on the faces of the elders. It was most unusual for anyone to appear uninvited at these important gatherings, and never a youth. "Be off with you," one said, and added a little pompously, "We have no time for foolishness; we are deciding important matters, such as how much grain to send to the capital for trade and how much to keep."

"But that is what I want to talk to you about," exclaimed Tan. "I am filled with unease over this sixth great harvest." The leader could not repress a laugh. The other elders put up their hands to hide their smiles. Tan, the dreamer, the least dependable young man in the village, filled with unease? Who could be concerned that Tan was filled with unease? Especially after such a great harvest.

But Tan gathered his courage and continued. "Did not Fu Hsi tell us that nothing goes straight up forever? Do we not see that every road has its turning, and every plain, its slope? According to the law of cyclic reversion, we should now be preparing for a severe winter, followed by an oppressive summer drought. We should therefore not trade any of our harvest but store it all away."

As Tan spoke, the smiles disappeared, and the elders looked at one another apprehensively, as if they had just been reminded of an important piece of information. The elders were good men and wise, and although they had only disdain for Tan, they looked at each other and nodded, and the leader spoke. "Thank you for your timely warning, young man. We will consider what you have said. You may go now."

The elders conferred, but could not agree whether the five great harvests in a row, capped by this prodigious sixth harvest, meant that the coming winter would be severe; possibly even as severe as the winter their grandfathers had told them of, the winter that had nearly destroyed everyone in the village.

After long discussion, one elder rose and spoke slowly, "I would remind you that the time is near for sending eight of our young men to Fu Hsi that he may select one to whom he will pass on the great wisdom. Surely, it would be appropriate for the eight young men we send to Fu Hsi to ask about the severity of the coming winter, and the seven not selected could bring back the answer."

The other elders were pleased with the suggestion, and so it was agreed that the selection process to choose the eight young men would begin immediately.

There had been great excitement when the villagers were first told of Fu Hsi's request, and although the villagers had tried to be modest, everyone was very proud that among so many villages, theirs had been the one chosen by the great Fu Hsi to provide him with his disciple. In the households where eligible young men lived, the excitement had been high all summer, for to have a son chosen as a potential disciple to the revered Fu Hsi was to provide that family with a place of honor in the village such as they could not hope to achieve in any other way.

Now that the time of choosing was at hand, the villagers could think of nothing else. For twenty days the elders held conferences with the ablest young men of the village, asking questions of them to determine their qualifications and seeking references from the other villagers about their conduct. Fully two hundred young men were interviewed.

During the entire selection period, Tan attempted again and again to be interviewed, but each time he was rebuffed, one or another of the elders telling him that his aimless and unproductive ways were well known to them, that only the finest and most reliable of the young men were being considered. Tan's parents appeared before the elders, and they were given the few minutes that all parents were entitled to. They began by acknowledging their son's aimless ways, but they also told the elders of his unnatural ability with plants and flowers, with animals and young children, of his uncanny ability to occasionally see future events, of his great memory, and of his protection and care of the older villagers. The elders listened politely, but then dismissed Tan's parents, and the next candidate was called in.

The choice of candidates was narrowed to twenty, then to ten, and, finally, the select eight were chosen. Tan was not among them.

He fell into a deep depression. His disappointment was so great that he couldn't speak even to his beloved parents. How he berated himself for the lost days that he had spent in wandering the hills, shirking his duties. If only he could live those days over, how diligently he would attend to his chores. No one would be more conscientious than he. But, alas, that was not to be; he had lost his opportunity.

Although he had a fierce desire to see the great Fu Hsi, to hear him speak, to be in the great sage's presence, there was something even greater than his desire that stirred inside him; he felt a distinct pull, a physical sensation drawing him toward the distant hills, and not to be able to respond to that pull was torture. It seemed impossible to him that he had not been chosen to go.

The day after the selections were completed, the chosen young men were given detailed directions for finding Fu Hsi, provisions for the ten-day journey, and, for the great sage, gifts of grains, furs, two milking goats, and five skins of their finest rice wine.

The eight young men left early the next morning, bound for the high mountains where Fu Hsi lived in quiet contemplation and seclusion. Fu Hsi—the very name filled them with awe. Every child in China was taught how Fu Hsi had come down from his beloved mountains seventy years before, speaking words of such great wisdom that he had been able to unite all of China, becoming her first emperor. They were told that his golden rule had brought forty years of peace and prosperity to the land, and that during the time of his inspired leadership, Fu Hsi had led them from the age of hunting and fishing into the age of planting crops, teaching them how to lay out their land in the magic nine-square form with the common well in the center. But his greatest ability, the one everyone spoke to their children of in hushed tones, was his ability to see into the future; to predict events and changes of every nature.

They told the children of how, on his one hundredth birthday, he had delegated the rulership of China to his eldest son, telling him that he was returning to his beloved solitude in the distant mountains because he had more important work to do.

Those were the stories told the length and breadth of China, but in the little village where Tan lived they also told the story that after Fu Hsi returned to his mountain home, he began to take a special interest in the little village that lay at the base of the mountain; their village. The children were told how the great sage watched over their days from afar but was as aware of their activities as if he lived among them; how he guided them, gave them good counsel, and was the final arbiter in any dispute that the people could not settle among themselves.

The villagers considered Fu Hsi to be their great treasure, and one for which they gave thanks daily. Now that Fu Hsi was to choose his first disciple from among them, that was glory indeed; an act that would gave their village a place of honor above all others for all time.

As the eight hopeful young men made their way through the forest, far to the rear where no one could see him, walked Tan, his meager supplies wrapped in an old cloth slung over his shoulder, a look of determination on his face. He knew that if it was discovered that he had disobeyed the elders and gone on the journey, he faced expulsion from the village and separation from his parents, but even though he did not know why he was going, he knew that he had to go.

CHAPTER TWO

Remembering

On a straw mat, in his small but well constructed house which nestled on the south facing side of the great mountains, sat Fu Hsi, fifty yarrow stalks held in his hand. He was old—very, very old. Silvery whiskers flowed down from his upper lip and chin, reaching nearly to his waist. His sparse, silvery hair was drawn straight back and gathered in a bun. His hands and face were slightly tanned, deeply lined, the skin nearly transparent. His eyes were bright and lively, and although his teeth were yellowed with age, he still had them all.

Having seen more than one hundred forty winters, he had decided this year that after he passed along his great wisdom to the chosen one, he would leave his body, allowing it to return to the earth to mix forever with the elements.

He had divined that the small group was coming, knew they would reach him in ten days at the fourth double hour after sunrise, knew their question, knew the answer, and most importantly, knew that among them was the person to whom he would pass along his vast store of knowledge, particularly that knowledge of the three-line and six-line figures that enabled him to see into the future and know all things.

Fu Hsi was sitting in the lotus position, his eyes closed, the tip of his tongue touching the back of his mouth, his breathing slowed almost to the point of cessation, the yarrow stalks forgotten in his hand as his thoughts flowed backward in time, back to the time when he was young, back to the time when he had discovered the way the universe communicated itself to him. Even then Fu Hsi's great intellect had penetrated deeply into the rhythms of the universe, had discovered that he was as much a part of the universe as all the stars he beheld, as much as the earth he walked, as much as the heaven of which he conceived.

Fu Hsi had known that some part of him was at one with "All-That-Is," which was the way he referred to the totality of existence and, as such, knew everything there was to know. He had been certain that if he could get in touch with the part of himself that knew everything, he could know the answer to any question and act without ever making a mistake.

The desire to be able to communicate with "the living essence of all that existed" was a fierce flame that burned mightily within his breast. Even then, he had visited this place where he now lived, on the south-facing side of the great mountain, preferring its quiet solitude to the activity of the villages.

One evening, the young Fu Hsi sat before his fire, concentrating deeply. The water to cook his rice was heating in a beautiful tortoise shell that was propped over his fire on some rocks. For several cycles of the moon, he had been silently turning over in his mind the question: "Should I withdraw from society completely to become a hermit, spending my days in the solitary contemplation of my questions about existence?" The alternative was to go back into the city, learn a trade, and take up a life among men.

So deep was his concentration that he failed to notice that the water in the tortoise shell had begun to boil, had boiled until it had all evaporated. Deprived of the cooling effect of the water, the shell finally cracked with a sharp sound. Startled from his contemplation, Fu Hsi saw that there was a great crack in the tortoise shell that traversed its entire bottom in one unbroken line.

He sat up, completely alert, his nerve endings tingling. Had not this same thing happened four times before when he was deep in concentration over a question and had forgotten to tend his boiling water? And each time had not a great crack appeared in the bottom of the shell? And had not two of the cracks gone completely across the bottom of the shell in an unbroken line, as this one had, and had not two of the cracks been separated in the middle by a small part of the shell that had remained whole? Could it be that the cracks had meaning for him, coming as they did when he was pondering questions of great importance? Could it be, he wondered, that All-That-Is was speaking to him in its own language?

Fu Hsi leaned against the rock behind him, his pulses racing, and looked up at the full moon, recalling each question he had been pondering each time a tortoise shell had cracked. The first time was two winters earlier when he was wondering whether the great rains would come that spring; the second time was in the summer of the same year when he was wondering whether the old man who had been struck on the head by the falling rock would die from his wound; the third time was the winter before when he had been wondering whether the village at the mouth of the great river would be invaded by its neighboring village; and the fourth time was just that summer when he was wondering whether the moon would be completely darkened over during its next cycle. Each question could have been answered "yes" or "no."

Fu Hsi remembered those questions, the subsequent events that revealed the answers to those questions, and what the cracks in the tortoise shells looked like on each occasion. Excitedly, he leaned forward and examined the shell. If the cracks were not just happenstance, if they had meaning for him, then from what he had earlier learned, the unbroken cracks meant "yes," and the broken cracks meant "no." If that were the case, this last cracking of the shell with its unbroken line meant nothing less than that he was destined to remain on the side of this mountain, pursuing his cherished dream of learning how to communicate with All-That-Is.

Quickly, he went to his storage area for another shell, which he propped over the glowing coals but this time without putting water into it. He held the question in his mind, "Do the cracks that occur in the shells have meaning?" Eagerly he waited, repeating the question in his mind. Suddenly, the shell cracked, and Fu Hsi, peering into the shell, saw that the crack traversed the entire bottom in one unbroken line. "Yes," he said in a whisper. Getting his last two shells, he put one over the coals, asking silently in his mind, "Does the broken line mean 'no' and the unbroken line mean 'yes'?" Again he waited, and again the shell cracked, and again the crack traversed its entire bottom in one unbroken line.

Almost feverishly excited now, he took his last shell, and disregarding the fact that after it cracked he would be unable to cook his rice, took a deep breath of the cool night air and placed it over the coals, asking aloud, "Is this daytime?" Anticipating a broken line that would indicate a "no" answer, he was unprepared for the sudden explosion that broke the shell into hundreds of tiny pieces. Fu Hsi fell back against the rock, nearly speechless. What could that mean? Then he laughed delightedly and sat forward exclaiming, "So, you will not answer frivolous questions or allow yourself to be tested."

Filled with a profound sense of gratitude, he knelt and bowed low until his forehead pressed the earth. He remained in that position for some time, breathing in the delightful scent of the earth, thinking how wonderful everything was, how perfect. Then he sat up and said aloud to the empty space around him, "I am eternally grateful to you for revealing yourself to me." He brushed a few grains of dirt from his forehead and returned to his rock. Leaning back, he said with a smile, "And I am happy to discover that you have a sense of humor."

In the years that followed, he asked many questions and received many answers, all of which were proved accurate by later events.

As it became ever more difficult to find a supply of tortoise shells, Fu Hsi wondered whether there was something else he could use other than tortoise shells. One evening he propped a shell over his cooking fire and asked, "Is there another way of asking questions besides heating tortoise shells?" Sitting in the lotus position with his eyes closed, he pondered his question deeply. Then he heard the cracking of the shell, and when he saw the unbroken crack across the bottom, he smiled.

After the passage of much time and the asking of many questions regarding other methods of making inquiries, Fu Hsi finally asked whether he could make inquiries using the stalks of plants. He sighed a deep sigh of relief when the unbroken crack appeared. The difficulty was that there were so many plants from which to choose.

One day, in the fall of the year, he was walking through a field where yarrow, sometimes called milfoil, grew abundantly. As he looked about him at the dried out plants, he felt a prickly sensation at the back of his neck, and his heart beat a little faster. He reached out and snapped one off at its base and examined it. The stalk was about two feet long and had a crown of small brown flowers that had dried forming a flat cluster. Thin branches from twelve to eighteen inches in length grew out from the side of the plant. In the spring and summer its flowers are white and its abundant green leaves are small and feathery, their frilly edges having a tendency to curl.

It had long been known that the dried flowers of the yarrow plant, when steeped in hot water, made an excellent cold remedy, and that the cooled yarrow water was good for bathing the face of people with oily skin and, when put into a gourd and used as a douche, for healing swollen tissues of the anal opening. Its round stalk, about a quarter of an inch thick at the base, usually grew straight, and when dried, was light and strong.

Fu Hsi snapped off a double armload of the stalks near their base and took them home. That evening he made a tea of some of the dried flowers, and after he had drunk the tea, he quieted himself and, putting a tortoise shell over his fire, asked whether yarrow was the plant he was to use.

He emitted a deep sigh of satisfaction when the shell said, "Yes."

There remained only the problem of finding out how to use the yarrow stalks to answer his questions.

Fu Hsi laid a stack of the stalks before him and began to study the stalks and handle them. He stripped them of all their leaves and branches.

Observing that the stalks were at various stages of dryness, he selected the ones that were the driest because they had a better feel and set the others aside. There remained in front of him about two hundred stalks. Some of the stalks were of different lengths, and he picked up some of the longer ones and passed them from hand to hand. Putting those stalks down he repeated the action with the shorter ones. He broke stalks to still other lengths and found definite satisfaction with a length that was about three times the width of his palm. When he held one vertically with his hand around the middle, the same length protruded above and below his hand.

After he had broken perhaps one hundred stalks to that length, Fu Hsi thought the stalks might be smoother, so he rubbed one stalk against another. After several periods of rubbing, he had a pleasing stack of smooth, dry stalks of about the same width and height, each one fairly straight. Every time he handled the stalks, he felt that he came a little closer to understanding their spirit.

Early the next morning, Fu Hsi sat with his yarrow stack at his left. He reached down and grasped a good portion of the stalks with his left hand. As he raised his hand, one of the stalks slipped from his grasp and fell onto the mat in front of him. The stalk seemed to be pointing at him, and he inquired, "Have you positioned yourself to watch me so that I do all right things and no wrong things?" After looking at the stalk for a few moments, Fu Hsi said, "Yes, I believe that is your role. From now on, whenever I use these stalks, you will be the observer stalk."

Fu Hsi then counted the stalks in his hand. There were forty-nine—seven sevens. Perhaps it would be necessary to go through seven steps or to work with seven stalks at a time. He took the forty-nine stalks back into his left hand, closed his eyes, breathed in deeply, and with his right hand, grasped a portion of the stalks, laid them on the mat in front of him and counted them. Twenty-four stalks. Nothing to do with seven. He tried it again. Eighteen stalks. Perhaps the number seven was not a factor.

Fu Hsi put all the stalks on the mat and looked at them. "Somewhere here in front of me," he said, "is the answer. Speak to me, little stalks." He separated the stalks into nine groups of five and one of four. He did not see a system or a method, but he saw that separating the stalks in some systematic way would result in certain numbers. Using the tortoise shells produced two different kinds of lines: broken and unbroken. Perhaps he should assign numbers to each kind of line and see if he could perceive a way of dividing the stalks so that the resulting numbers would tell him which kind of line was the answer. The more he handled the stalks, the better they felt. He knew that it would take time to discover how to use them, but he knew he would find the answer. He closed his eyes and entered the void thinking, "What a joyous task."

Within the next few years Fu Hsi not only learned how to use the yarrow stalks, he also learned to combine the broken and unbroken lines, then to add more lines; finally, he was able to conceive of an entire system, a miniature model of All-That-Is, complete with all its stages of change. Then he was able to know the future; neither far nor near, neither dark nor deep was hidden from him. He could see into the heart of all things. By the time he finished asking questions, learning the ways of heaven and earth, forty more years had passed, and he was ready to pass his vast knowledge on to the first messenger who would carry it to the next and he to the next and the knowledge would not pass from the earth. Fu Hsi had seen it.

Fu Hsi's thoughts returned to the present and to the arrival of the young villagers.

CHAPTER THREE
The Arrival

At the fourth double hour after sunrise, Fu Hsi was standing on a platform that extended from the side of his house. Below the platform was a sheer drop of a thousand feet. Sandalwood incense burned on either side of him, and from where he stood he could see the little band of young men climbing upward along the path that led to his house.

He made his way slowly inside the house using a gnarled ebony staff. The six-foot staff, a gift given to him while he was still emperor by a prince from a far off land, was as black as obsidian, and nearly as hard, and it was burnished until it shone as if with an inner light. He seated himself on a cushion on a raised platform in front of an altar upon which burned more incense. His silken robe hung from his shoulders and cascaded down like flowing gold to the straw mat upon which the cushion lay.

That is where the little band of young men found him. They approached on their knees, and when they saw him, they bowed low, their foreheads touching the ground, their arms outstretched before them. Fu Hsi tapped the floor with his staff. They looked up cautiously, and he gestured for them to come and sit before him. They were awed by his presence. Their eyes were opened as wide as possible, and they crept forward timidly and sat on the small cushions that were positioned in front of the raised platform. None of them had ever seen him before, but from the time they were small children, all had heard the stories of this greatest of all sages.

Outside, Tan wriggled and squirmed his way through the flowers and bushes until he lay behind a small bush less than twenty feet from the house. He could see the open doorway, and he was close enough to hear what was said. Parting the branches of the bush allowed him to see Fu Hsi, and his heart quaked as the great sage greeted the young men.

Fu Hsi looked over the group with eyes that seemed to shine with an inner light. He knew that among them was the one who would carry the sacred knowledge forward, for had he not divined it in his readings of the yarrow stalks?

The first time he had consulted the oracle regarding his successor, he received the symbols of "lake" over "Earth"

Therefore, a lake on the Earth, which is a collection of water: the symbol of "gathering together." Fu Hsi knew that in the time of gathering together there were secret forces at work, leading together those who belonged together. He knew that he did not have to make any arbitrary choice among the eight young men, that the chosen one would be revealed to him in an obvious way. The next reading had shown him that the person lived in the village at the foot of his mountain, and that he was a young man. Other readings had informed him that the young man was not too modest, but he was intelligent, black-haired, tall, dark-eyed, and that he was considerate of children and older people.

What intrigued Fu Hsi about the young man was that he was a dreamer, a person who wandered the hills, often not tending to his duties. Fu Hsi smiled as he remembered his own distant youth, and how much alike he and this young man were.

Fu Hsi asked their names and listened intently as each told him his name in a tremulous voice. He then asked each of them in turn why he wanted to become his disciple, and then other questions of a personal nature. He asked whether they had brothers and sisters, what they did when there was no work to be done, whether they liked music, and what skills they possessed.

As he listened to them answer each question in turn, he began to feel uneasy. Something was amiss. He had expected to perceive immediately which one was to be his disciple. Something did not feel right. He dismissed them, telling them what their various duties were for the rest of the day and evening, and where they were to sleep.

Tan crept away into hiding, longing to be part of what was unfolding, but very much afraid to be discovered, fearing he would be turned into a rat or an owl or sent away with a reprimand to the village elders.

Early the next morning, after the young men ate their rice and drank their tea, Fu Hsi led them to an open glade in the forest a short distance from his house. He seated himself on a rock shaped like a chair while the young men seated themselves in a half circle in front of him on straw mats. Then Fu Hsi continued to ask them about themselves: their duties at home, their families, what they thought about life, animals, love, marriage, children, elder people, and what each knew of the world around him. Fu Hsi asked one question at a time, and the young men answered in turn until all had spoken ten times, completing a full cycle.

Fu Hsi tilted his head back and looked up at the sky. He was more perplexed than the day before. None of them seemed to be the one he was seeking. But how could that be? He had seen from his inquiries that this was the time for the chosen one to appear, that he lived in the village at the foot of his mountain, that he would be among the group that was here. During his questioning, Fu Hsi came to see that these young men had been chosen by the village elders because of their attention to their duties, because they could be depended upon to fulfill their chores, because of their reliability, but Fu Hsi's divinations had shown him that the person he was seeking was neglectful of his duties, and not very dependable at all, except when children, older people, or animals were concerned. Yet he knew that the one he was seeking was here; he must be here; the readings were unerringly accurate.

During the questioning, Tan lay hidden behind a large rock, listening. He was filled with dismay as he heard the proud answers the other young men gave to Fu Hsi's questions. How he now regretted his aimless ways. How he wished with all his heart that he had not neglected his duties, had not wandered off into the fields when he had been assigned chores. How he longed to be the chosen one, to be able to sit at the feet of this greatest of all sages and drink in his words. Tan felt himself an arid desert that cried out for that spring of pure wisdom which was waiting to be poured forth like a stream of sparkling fresh water from an inexhaustible spring, where he, Tan, would thirstily drink it in and make it his own.

He crept away to where he had left his pack, put his head down, and wept. Never had he been so sad. From the first moment he had seen Fu Hsi just after the young men arrived, he had felt an ache within himself just to be in the great man's presence. Never had he felt anything like that emotion. Before that moment he had at most felt a mild admiration even for the most respected men of the village. But now, in the presence of the fabled Fu Hsi, the greatest sage China had ever known, it seemed as if every cell in his body was crying out for Fu Hsi's wisdom. It had taken all his will to restrain himself from running into the little house and prostrating himself on the floor, begging to be allowed just to listen.

After the evening meal, Fu Hsi, determined to find the answer to this puzzle, led the way back to the clearing and began questioning the young men again, but this time, not in any fixed order. Tan again lay secreted behind the big rock. Fu Hsi pointed with his ebony staff to the night sky and asked the group, "When you look up at the stars, do any of you see anything that looks like a recognizable shape?" Silence. Each man in the little group looked around at his neighbors to see if anyone had an answer. No one spoke. Fu Hsi peered at them from under his silver eyebrows, his long staff clasped in his hand, his hair and beard glistening in the moonlight.

Tan squirmed behind his rock, nearly bursting with his need to respond. Had he not lain on the hills for hundreds of hours imagining all sorts of pictures made up of the stars? Had he not seen what he imagined to be swords, bulls, spiders, animals of all sorts, and small groups of stars that seemed to belong to secret societies. He wanted to leap into the circle and point upwards exclaiming, "Look! There! Can you not see the scorpion? His great tail arched over his back? And there! Do you not see the broad belt with the long sword in it? And there, that cluster of stars I call 'The Sisters?'" But he lay behind his rock, clasping his knees tightly, afraid to reveal himself.

"Tell me," Fu Hsi said, "does anyone here have any idea why the snake sheds his skin, or why the baby deer are born with spots, or why the birds fly south in the fall?" Tan quivered with excitement. Had he not thought of answers to every one of those questions and hundreds more like them? Had not everyone? Silence from the group. Then one young man timidly raised his hand. Fu Hsi nodded, inviting him to speak.

"I do not know the answers to your questions," he said, "but there is one back in our village who might possibly know those answers."

"Who might that be?" inquired Fu Hsi, his interest brightening.

"His name is Tan," said the young man. Several of the others snorted derisively and shook their heads. One laughed aloud. Fu Hsi noted their reactions, his interest quickening. In back of his rock, Tan squirmed with embarrassment.

"Why is he not among you?" asked Fu Hsi.

"He wanted to come; he tried for days," said the young man. "His mother and father gave evidence before the council, but the elders wouldn't consider it. I overheard one of them say that Tan is the last person in the village he would think of sending." And then he added in a low voice, as if he were trying to amuse his friends, "He said he'd rather send a cow."

There were titters of laughter from the other young men. Fu Hsi smiled inwardly and nodded, thinking how just it was, how fitting, that the lad whom the elders considered least in the village, for whom they had no regard, no respect, the one that even his peers regarded with disdain, was probably the one he was seeking, the messenger to whom he would pass along the great wisdom.

Listening to the young man's words and hearing the snorts of derision from his peers, Tan crouched down lower behind the rock, his face burning with shame. Tears of anguish coursed down his cheeks. Only his fear of being seen prevented him from fleeing, but he resolved that the moment the group broke and went back to the house, he would leave that place, never to return.

Fu Hsi nodded and lowered his head almost sadly. Of course, he should have known that when he sent his request to the village for young men, that they would only send the choicest among the young men, never considering that a dreamer would be the one he was seeking. But what of his readings? Why wasn't the lad here? He had never been misled before. Why now? He closed his eyes and leaned on his staff.

As he sat there, Fu Hsi's vast intellect directed itself toward the symbols of "gathering together." He had absolute confidence in the all-powerful forces he knew to be at work in heaven and on earth. He breathed in fully and exhaled slowly, allowing the rhythm of All-That-Is to penetrate deep within his being, to carry him, to mold him, to bring him thoughts from the very source of everything, from the One. His breathing slowed, his heartbeat slowed, he seemed to withdraw into himself, and in his stillness, he smiled. The words repeated themselves in his mind: "In the time of 'gathering together' it is not necessary to make any arbitrary choice of your comrades; there are secret forces at work, leading together those who belong together." Fu Hsi knew that the person he was seeking was not one of the young men in front of him. He also knew that the person would come—would come as inevitably as the snows in winter, as the new leaves in the spring. He sank deeper into himself, into the void, into All-That-Is, and still with his eyes closed, he shook his head slowly. "No," he thought, "that is not quite right; the person is here; he is here now—he must be."

Fu Hsi stood up. The young men, taking his action to mean that the questioning was over, also stood up. But Fu Hsi just stood there, his head cocked to one side, as if he were listening.

A night bird called from the southeast: two short notes, then a long one, the sign of northwest. Fu Hsi took a few small steps in that direction, leaned on his staff and paused. Another bird call came: three short notes, the sign of the north. He altered his course slightly and walked a few steps in that direction, then paused again. A branch snapped in the forest, ever so slightly to the east of the direction in which he was headed. He smiled slightly, and, almost holding his breath in his concentration, moved toward the sound. When he was at the edge of the clearing, he stopped. He was directly in front of the rock behind which lay Tan. Fu Hsi bowed his head, both hands holding his staff as he leaned on it, and waited. He took a deep breath and held it. The eight young men looked at each other uncertainly. What was happening? What were they witnessing?

The bird call sounded, this time from high up in a tree almost directly over Fu Hsi's head: one long screech. Fu Hsi slowly exhaled, as if in relief; then he nodded his head in understanding, as if he had been spoken to, walked around the rock and looked down at the huddled figure who lay there, looking up at him fearfully. Fu Hsi leaned on his staff and smiled. "You must be Tan," he said. "Welcome. I've been waiting for you."

CHAPTER FOUR

The First Teaching

Early the next morning the eight young men departed with Fu Hsi's kind words for them and messages for the elders, including a warning to save their harvest and prepare for a severe winter followed by a long drought.

For the next two days Tan was in a continual state of bliss, watching the old man move about or sit or speak. To be in his presence was a supreme delight. He had heard from the ancient sage about the young Fu Hsi's absentmindedness that led to the boiling away of the water and the subsequent cracking of the shells. He felt comforted to know that his revered master possessed some of the same qualities he himself had so recently berated himself for having. He laughed when Fu Hsi told him how one of the shells had exploded, and even before Fu Hsi told him what he believed it had meant, Tan perceived the meaning and blurted out his thoughts. Fu Hsi was pleased. There was much to tell, and that Tan was so quick to perceive the subtleties would allow the work to proceed rapidly.

They were in a cool grove of pine trees at the rear of the house. Nearby rose the great rocks of the mountain. From a fissure in the rocks flowed a sparkling rivulet of icy water. It glittered and splashed as it fell in a tiny waterfall to a small pool below from whence it continued its journey along a stream bed of small rocks. The wonder-filled, magical sound of the flowing water made Tan believe that the water goddess herself was serenading them. In the pool, a skin of fresh goat's milk lay cooling.

With his ebony staff, Fu Hsi drew two lines in the dirt in front of them. One, an unbroken line (—), and the other, a broken line (– –). "The unbroken line means 'yes,'" said Fu Hsi, "and the broken line means 'no.' In the beginning, and for many years, that was all I perceived, but I was consumed with the need to know the answers to questions that could be answered with more than just 'yes' or 'no.'

Later, I put the two lines together and so had four combinations." As he spoke he continued to draw lines in the dirt with the tip of his staff. "The two unbroken lines, one over the other (═), meant 'absolutely yes,' or 'emphatically yes.' " Fu Hsi drew two broken lines, one over the other (= =).

"And the two broken lines," said Tan excitedly, looking up into the old man's eyes, "meant 'absolutely no,' or 'emphatically no.' "

Fu Hsi nodded, and asked as he drew two more lines, "And the unbroken line under a broken line (==), what does that mean?"

"That means 'probably yes' or 'probably no'; I can't figure out which." Tan's quick answer brought a smile to Fu Hsi's face. Tan was an even better student than he had hoped for.

"To know which," said the master, "look into nature and see how things grow. Does that help you?"

Tan thought for a moment. He imagined grass growing, flowers, a tree, then, a seed lying in the ground, awaiting its summons from above. Tan nodded slowly, understandingly, and he looked up at the old man's face that radiated energy and warmth, just as did the sun. "It seems," said Tan hesitatingly, "that as the plants and trees grow from below, so also the pair of lines would grow from below, and therefore would take their meaning from the lower of the two lines. That means that the unbroken line under the broken line (==) means 'probably yes,' and the broken line under the unbroken line (==) means 'probably no.' " Fu Hsi could hardly keep the expression of pleasure from his face. How perceptive this young man was.

"Yes," said Fu Hsi, "that is correct, or it could mean 'moderately' yes or no, depending on your question." Tan looked puzzled. Fu Hsi explained: "Suppose you wanted to know whether the coming winter would be severe or mild, and you received the answer of an unbroken line under a broken line (⚍), what would that mean?"

Understanding broke over Tan's face. "It would mean that we would have a moderately mild winter."

Fu Hsi slapped his staff lightly with the flat of his fingers as he sometimes did, indicating applause, then he nodded, stood up, and walked from the pine grove to the platform at the side of his house. He frequently changed the environment for their talks so that the information would not seem to be an endless stream but would be accentuated by location changes. He also changed the tone of his voice and the volume with which he spoke. Sometimes he spoke reflectively, at other times assertively. Sometimes he spoke softly, occasionally loudly, at other times in a whisper. The delivery of the information was varied and thus impressed itself deeply into the mind of Tan.

On the platform, they settled themselves on cushions, their backs against the wall of the house. In front of them were the sacred mountains, the far off plains, and the shining river, a meandering silver line in the distance. Between them, on the wooden planks of the porch, was a beautiful tortoise shell, twenty inches across, filled with powdery, gray dust. Blocks of wood pushed under its sides, prevented it from moving.

Tan asked, "Master, when the tortoise shells cracked, what was happening? Was the tortoise shell God talking to you?"

"I used to believe the stories I heard as a child," replied Fu Hsi. "The same stories you probably heard. I was told that there are many Gods, a God of the river, a God of the mountains, a God of the sun, a God of the animals, and so on. Now I believe that there is just one supreme intelligence that was and is responsible for everything. I believe that everything that exists is made up of the very substance of that Supreme Intelligence, and that we and everything else are all one."

"One God?" thought Tan. "Impossible!" His mouth fell open in incredulity. Yet, the great Fu Hsi had just told him so.

The first night after he had been selected as the chosen one, he had lain on his sleeping mat and pondered deeply over what he imagined might lay in store for him. He expected he would hear many things from Fu Hsi that were far removed from anything he had ever heard before, or even of which he had conceived. He had therefore resolved that no matter what he heard from the great old man, he would believe it, that he would put his trust in the venerable sage completely. But one God? Over everything? And even more unbelievable, he, Tan, was part of that God?

Fu Hsi smiled, acknowledging the boy's effort of will not to cry out at what, for him, must be a staggering bit of information. He reached over and gently pushed Tan's chin up, closing his mouth. Tan laughed at his own stupefaction as Fu Hsi continued.

"When I held the questions in my mind during the heating of the tortoise shells, because I am one with everything, as you are, as everyone and everything is, including the tortoise shells, I influenced the cracking of the shells. The shells and I and you and everyone else are all made of the same essence from the same source—we are inseparably connected. Had I not been thinking of those questions, or had I been thinking of different questions, the shells may have cracked differently."

Forgetting his resolve not to question but to simply absorb, Tan exclaimed, "But surely the shells are not alive. They can't think—they can't know what you're thinking."

"The possibility is hard to conceive," replied Fu Hsi, "but think for a moment. If everything that was made, was made from the same God-substance, then everything has life: the animals, the trees, the distant stars, even the soil and the rocks themselves. We may not be able to perceive the life of a stone, but that does not mean that it does not live." Fu Hsi fell silent. Tan was absorbed in his thoughts, his mind stretching, reeling, reaching to see what Fu Hsi saw. He realized how little he knew, how much this ancient fount of wisdom knew. He saw himself at the beginning of what looked to be an endless journey. Without thinking, he shook his head, sadly. Fu Hsi, correctly interpreting the Tan's movement, nodded understandingly. He reached over and patted the young man's head. "Do not worry yourself. Before we finish, you will know all; I have seen it." Then he lapsed into silence to let Tan regain his balance.

CHAPTER FIVE

The Second Teaching

After an hour of silence Fu Hsi resumed from where they had left off. "I used those four original combinations of two lines each for many years, and with their aid I was able to add greatly to my knowledge. One day, I realized it was time to push out the boundaries of my little system. Through observation, I had learned that when male and female mate, whether it be people, animals, or plants, they produce another of their kind. Since the broken line and the unbroken line represent nothing less than male and female, to each of the four pairs of lines I added a broken line at the bottom to represent the female offspring (☴ ☵ ☶ ☵ ☷), and to each of the four pairs of lines I added an unbroken line at the bottom to represent the male offspring (☰ ☱ ☲ ☳). There were then eight different combinations." As he spoke, Fu Hsi drew lines in the dust of the tortoise shell to represent each of the eight figures, or symbols called *kua* (gwa).

Tan sat with his attention so focused on Fu Hsi's words and on the drawings that his breathing was nearly suspended. He still found it difficult to believe that he was there, that the great Fu Hsi, the most honored and revered sage in all of China, perhaps in all of the world, was actually speaking to him, and that he, Tan, was the chosen one; the one to whom the great knowledge was being passed along, for him to give to his children, and they to their children. He felt so honored by it all that he was in a continual state of gratitude, a fact that was not lost on his teacher.

"Because," Fu Hsi continued, "the lines are male and female, I soon came to know that the eight kua, taken all together, represented 'the family.' Can you tell me what members of the family are represented by each of the kua?"

Tan nodded, as if in a trance, and spoke as if the words were not his own but were coming through him from some ethereal being. His voice sounded cracked because in his intense concentration he had not swallowed even once, and his throat had become dry. Pointing to the lines in the dust that Fu Hsi had drawn, he said, "The three unbroken lines (☰) represent the father, and the three broken lines (☷), the mother." Fu Hsi nodded but said nothing. Tan continued. "Since everything that grows comes from below and grows upward, including the lines, and since the unbroken line is male, that means the first or oldest son would be this one."

Tan pointed to the three line figure in the dust that showed an unbroken line under two broken lines (☳). He looked at Fu Hsi expectantly who nodded. "That means," continued Tan, pointing at the figure of a broken line under two unbroken lines (☴), "that this figure stands for the first or eldest daughter."

Fu Hsi again nodded and then pointed to the figure that showed an unbroken line between two broken lines (☵) asking, "And this one?"

Tan thought for a moment, then said hesitantly, "I don't know. If you had asked me what this one was," he pointed to the figure of two unbroken lines under a broken line (☱), "I would have said it was the middle son because the lines grow from the bottom, and so the next son would be another unbroken line."

Fu Hsi looked approvingly at Tan and said, "That is what I, too, thought at first, but after working with the kua for several years, I perceived that such is not the case. The unbroken line that appears in the middle (☵) is not a second unbroken line that grows up from the first line, but is the same line that has moved up one space."

Tan nodded and said, "I understand." He thought for a moment, then a smile brightened his face. "Then," said Tan, "it must be that when the unbroken line moves up another space to the top (☶), it gives the meaning of the youngest son. The same must be true for the broken lines with regard to the daughters." He pointed at the kua as he spoke. "The broken line under two unbroken lines (☴) stands for the oldest daughter, the broken line between two unbroken lines (☲) stands for the middle daughter, and the broken line over two unbroken lines (☱) represents the youngest daughter." Fu Hsi smiled so beautifully that for Tan the sun seemed to have risen.

Tan studied the eight kua, his brow furrowed in concentration. They seemed to burn themselves into his mind. Fu Hsi reached out and smoothed the dust with his hand, covering the kua. "Now," he said, "draw the eight kua again, and tell me what each stands for." Tan did as he was instructed. Fu Hsi smiled and nodded. "Now," he said, "it is time for tea and rice. Do you know how to prepare tea?"

"Yes," exclaimed Tan, leaping to his feet, "I prepared tea in the village for the older folks who had difficulty in caring for themselves. They said I was the best tea-maker in the village."

Fu Hsi glanced piercingly up at the young man, and the light in his eyes flashed lightning. Tan shrunk within himself. "Modesty," said Fu Hsi severely, "is to be prized in a man above all other qualities. The man who boasts of himself is like a rooster crowing in the fields; he invites the fox. It is human nature to despise the boaster and to love the man of modesty."

Tan hung his head, his face flaming with his embarrassment. He fell to his knees and, bowing until his forehead touched the wooden planks of the porch, pleaded, "Forgive me, please, great master. I am worth less than nothing. I will not eat for three days in penance for my shortcomings. Please, take your great staff and beat me with it, or I will not be able to live."

Fu Hsi looked at the young man, and his face softened. He reached over and touched Tan lightly on the shoulder with his hand, saying, "Sit up, my son. Your sincerity and humility are becoming to you. It is enough that you have received the lesson of modesty. Now, go and prepare the tea, and it will speak eloquently for you as a maker of tea."

CHAPTER SIX

The Return

The eight young men who had journeyed to see Fu Hsi were still a mile from home when they were seen by a farmer who ran all the way to the village to take the news that the small envoy was returning, and wonder of wonders, he exclaimed, all eight were returning.

By the time the eight men reached the village, a crowd had turned out to see them. On every tongue there were the questions: "What happened? Why are there eight of you? Did you find Fu Hsi? Did he reject all of you?" None of the eight said anything until they were in the center of the village. Then one, whom Fu Hsi had appointed spokesman, said, "We have a message for the chief elder. It is to him that we must speak first."

The chief elder was sent for. When he arrived, the spokesman said, "I am instructed by our revered master, Fu Hsi, to ask that you gather the council members and the villagers in the town square this evening. There I am to deliver Fu Hsi's message." The chief elder said not a word but nodded his head, bowed slightly, and left. What a stir there was in the village, what questions were put to the eight young men, but not a word would they say.

The parents of Tan sought out the spokesman, whose name was Ping and asked if he, or any of the other seven, had seen anything of their son who had been missing since they left.

Ping nodded and said, "Come to the meeting this evening, and you will know all. Until then I can say nothing."

"You saw our son? Is he all right? Has any harm befallen him? Please, speak, that we may know the worst immediately."

"Your son has not been harmed in any way. He is well, but I can say no more until this evening. Please do not ask me anything further."

"Oh, thank you, thank you!" said Tan's mother. "We will not ask you anything further but will wait with the others until tonight."

After the evening meal, everyone gathered at the center of the village. There was a fire burning in the pit, and the elders were seated on a platform. Everyone in the village had gathered. The eight young men were standing in front of the platform. Ping addressed the elders. "Fu Hsi has asked that I stand on the platform to deliver his message to our people. May I come up?"

There was an undercurrent of excited whispers that went through the villagers like wind. The elders looked at one another. The chief elder spoke. "We honor the request of the exalted Fu Hsi. You may come onto the platform."

Nervously, Ping ascended the steps and stood in front of the people of his village. He was frightened, and his first words were spoken haltingly, but then, as he concentrated on remembering what he was to say, his nervousness left him, and he spoke easily. "Our most revered master sends you his greetings. He personally thanks each and every one of you for giving your full attention to his request for eight disciples. Before I tell you about that, I am to tell you the answer to your question regarding the great harvest and the coming winter. Fu Hsi says that the coming winter will be severe, worse than any that the village has ever experienced. He urges each of us to store as much firewood as possible, and to store our grain. We are to keep all of it except what is needed to trade for other supplies.

"Because of this timely warning, we will be safe. There is nothing to fear. The long winter will be followed by a drought in the summer. Our crops will be meager. But again, because we have been warned, all will be well. We are to care for each other, to help him who does not have enough, or who needs aid. In this way, we will all be safe. So says our most revered sage, the honorable Fu Hsi."

He was silent then, and there arose a murmur from the crowd, blessing Fu Hsi. A voice cried from the rear, "It was Tan who saw what was coming. Tell us of Tan, have you seen him?"

"Yes," said Ping, "I have. That is the second part of my message. Tan has become Fu Hsi's disciple." The eyes of the elders darted from one to the other. Exclamations arose from the crowd. Tan, Fu Hsi's disciple! Hardly anyone besides Tan's parents could believe the young man's statement. Not that they doubted Ping's words; no, they knew him to be an honorable person, but what they knew of Tan strained their imaginations to the limit to think of him as the chosen one. Ping continued. "It is he to whom the great wisdom is being taught, and it is he who will teach it to his children, and they to theirs, and in that manner the great wisdom will continue through the ages from generation to generation."

All eyes sought Tan's mother and father. Those closest to the happy couple saw that Tan's mother was crying and that his father was holding her hand and smiling and nodding. Well-wishers were patting him on the back and saying how fortunate he was and how happy they were for him.

Ping held up his hand for silence. "Fu Hsi said that I am to tell you that the selection was not based upon merit, or character, or devotion to duty, or any particular ability. He said that the selection was made at the beginning of time, and that all the succeeding generations of wisdom keepers have also been so selected, each to take his place in the procession at the appointed time."

The villagers whispered questions: "How can Fu Hsi know? Tan? Who would have thought it? How can Fu Hsi know about the coming winter and the following summer?" Yet none doubted that Fu Hsi did know, and all were grateful.

Ping turned to the elders on the platform and said, "Fu Hsi sends you his greetings and says that you are to be commended for your masterful leadership of the village. He says that he will continue to watch over our village and give us guidance as it is needed." Turning to face the villagers he said, "Lastly, Fu Hsi said I was to say to the parents of Tan that he congratulates you for bringing up a fine son and he thanks you for watching over his disciple for him until the appointed time."

With those words, Fu Hsi elevated Tan's parents to the position of highest honor in the village. They turned to each other, then looked humbly to the ground. With hearts beating heavily, the father whispered, "Our son," and the mother whisper, "The chosen one."

CHAPTER SEVEN

The Third Teaching

One hundred meters east of Fu Hsi's house was a clearing in which the master had created a small garden. Late one afternoon, Fu Hsi was seated in this garden on the hollow trunk of a fallen tree. Around him grew a such a profusion of flowers and vegetables that it seemed as if nature had gone out of her way to show her love for the great sage. He tapped his staff against the trunk, and the sound reverberated through the area. Tan came running and threw himself down in front of Fu Hsi, his forehead touching the dirt. "Yes, great master, your servant is here. How can I be of service to you?"

Fu Hsi said sternly, "You can stop throwing yourself down in the dirt like that. Sit up, look at me."

Tan did as he was bidden. It was extremely difficult for him to look into his master's eyes. They were so alert and so piercing that they seemed to peer into his very soul. In a sudden insight, he knew that Fu Hsi could, in fact, see into his very being, that he could never hide anything from him or be anything other than completely forthright and truthful with this great master. Nor, Tan realized, did he want to be anything other than forthright with him. With that realization, he looked straight into the eyes of Fu Hsi, not so much to see but to allow what was within himself to be seen.

Fu Hsi gazed into the lad's eyes a long moment. Then he smiled a smile that lit up Tan's entire world, and he said, "Good, my son, very good." And he nodded, his long silvery beard and eyebrows glistening in the sun. "You are the first in what will be a long line of messengers who will carry the sacred wisdom to all humankind throughout the ages. This is where it begins. The wisdom I pass along to you will shape civilizations for as many years as there are trees on this mountain." Tan looked at the trees that grew from the mountain down to the plains, many miles below. "And not just the Chinese civilization but many others as well. Great men and women from all lands shall come to know of it and shall carry it back to their own lands."

"Will the wisdom remain the same, being passed along through so many messengers?"

"In the case of the messengers, yes, it will remain very much the same, but in the case of people who learn the wisdom, who are not themselves part of the long line of chosen messengers, no. It will be altered. It will form the basis for many religions, indeed, nearly all religions in all lands. After you have learned the essential aspects, I will teach you the wisdom in the form of a long poem which you will memorize."

Tan exclaimed, "I have an excellent mem—" He stopped short and looked at the ground, saying nothing. Fu Hsi went on as if Tan had not spoken. "It is the poem which you will pass along with the line figures. You hold an honored position, one which carries great responsibility. Therefore, you must at all times act with dignity."

Tan looked earnestly into the eyes of his revered teacher. "I understand Great Master; it shall be as you wish." And he sat up very straight. "Are we to continue now?"

"Yes," replied Fu Hsi. Tan took his seat, which was another log, but smaller, and looked inquiringly at his master. Fu Hsi nodded. Tan picked up a small stick, and in the dirt in front of them drew the eight kua. "The kua," said Fu Hsi, "stand for more than just members of the family; they also stand for all the forces that are at work in heaven and on earth. This one," he said, pointing to the figure of the father (☰), "stands for the creative force of God. Not God himself, but the force that God uses to bring everything that there is into being, to create. And not to create just those things that you can see and touch, but also those things that you cannot see or touch: ideas, thoughts, wind, sound, heat, cold, scents. It manifests itself as the male force; it is active and powerful. Do you understand?"

"Yes, master, I understand."

"And this one," said Fu Hsi, pointing to the three-line figure that represented the mother (☷), "stands for the receptive force of God. It is through the receptive force that the creative force creates. On its own, the creative force can do nothing. The receptive force is not the opposite of the creative force; it is the complement of it. Neither one is greater than the other. As the receptive force, it is like the earth; it is not the earth, but it is *like* the earth which brings forth all there is which is on the earth. It is passive and yielding. Together, the Creative and the Receptive bring into being the ten thousand things."

"The ten thousand things?"

"That is just another way of saying, 'All-That-Is.' Just as in our world where male and female mate and bring forth children, so the creative and the receptive mate and bring about the emergence of all else. If you wanted to make a figure out of clay, your desire is the creative force, and the clay is the receptive force—that from which you make the figure. Neither the creative nor the receptive can make the figure without the other. The female force is called 'the receptive' because it receives the energy of the male force."

"Do the kua have names?"

"Yes. The name of the father figure (☰) is 'Ch'ien.' (chee en) The name of the mother figure (☷) is 'K'un.' (kwen)"

"What about the other kua? What do they stand for?"

"This one," said Fu Hsi, pointing to the figure of the eldest son (☳), "stands for the arousing force, the force that makes things happen. Its name is 'Chên' (jen)."

"What do you mean it 'makes things happen?' I thought that the Ch'ien force made things happen."

"The Ch'ien force is the creative force that brings things into being; it creates. The Chên force arouses things into action once they have been created. It is the force that calls forth things that grow, the force that wakens you in the morning, the force that arouses you to action when you have an idea; it is the force that begins things; its symbol is thunder. It is not thunder, but it is like thunder in its outward aspects."

"Is there a force that stops things once they have started?"

"That is a good question and shows that you are thinking along the correct lines. Yes, there is a force that stops things; it is called 'Ken' (gen)." Fu Hsi pointed to the figure of the youngest son (☶). "It is symbolized by the mountain. It is not the mountain, but it is like the mountain in its outer aspects. It means 'quiet strength' and 'broad base.'"

Tan was eager for more, but Fu Hsi said that it was time for tea and rice. He said, "Use your Chên force to stir yourself to action and begin the tea preparation."

Tan laughed delightedly and jumped up to do as he was bidden, saying as he went, "Great Master, I shall not let the Ken force stop me until my task is completed." He bowed and left.

CHAPTER EIGHT

Seeing

Fu Hsi sat with his eyes closed. With his inner vision he looked into the far distant future. He knew that the information he was passing along to Tan would last as long as there were people on the Earth—many thousands of years beyond the current moment. He thought of all the successors who would come after him, each one a lover of wisdom, a seeker. He knew that some of them would be powerful and would become leaders of men; others would be scholars who loved wisdom for its own sake. All of them would be good men—men shaped by the wisdom they had learned from their predecessors, and they would all be dedicated to the preservation of the wisdom. Some of them, he knew, would give their lives so that the wisdom could be saved. How he loved them all; how he wished he could meet them all.

"Perhaps," he thought, "on the other side of the veil that separates me from the beyond, I shall meet them."

That the time was fast coming, he knew, and he smiled as he dozed off, the warm sun lighting his features. A beautiful butterfly alighted on his shoulder, its wings slowly opening and closing, as if fanning the sleeping sage.

CHAPTER NINE

The Fourth Teaching

After tea, they walked down the path that led from Fu Hsi's house to the plains below. Fu Hsi walked very slowly, leaning on his staff for support. Several hundred yards from the house there was a natural clearing that looked over the valley below. Two rocks near the edge of the clearing were chosen as the work area. Fu Hsi sat on one of the rocks and Tan on the other. Tan drew the eight kua in the dust with the tip of a short stick he had brought along for the purpose.

Fu Hsi pointed to the figure of the middle son (☵) and said, "This is K'an (cun), the symbol of the abyss and of water. The abyss stands for danger, as does water, which, as a flood or a tidal wave or a great storm, can also bring danger. The broken line on either side of the unbroken line stands for the sides of a ravine within which water, the unbroken line, is flowing." Tan nodded his head in understanding. Fu Hsi continued. "The middle daughter (☲), called Li (lee), stands for the sun or fire, also light and reason."

"Reason?" inquired Tan.

"Yes. Your ability to think, to understand. When you don't know something, it is like being in the dark; you can't see. When you find out that which you need to know, it is as if the light comes and banishes the darkness." Fu Hsi smiled. "Does that bring my young disciple the light of understanding?"

"Yes," said Tan, "it does. It is good for me to think of it that way because many times I have had the feeling that I was in the darkness when I did not know something. When I found out what I needed to know, it was as if the sun came out."

"Very good," said Fu Hsi, "that is exactly right. Now, this figure of the eldest daughter (☴) is called Sun (soon). Its symbol is wind, the gently penetrating wind that blows over the earth. It is not the wind, but it is like the wind in its outward aspects. You have, no doubt, seen rumors spread in your village?" Tan nodded. "That is the force of Sun at work. It is the disperser, like the wind that blows over the earth. When a message goes out from the chief elder to the villagers; it is the force of Sun that spreads the word. Even though you cannot see the force, you can see its effects. It is the same with the other forces. They themselves cannot be seen, but their effects can be seen. Sun has a secondary meaning: wood, wood that grows, such as a tree. Also, when Sun, as wood, pushes upward through the earth, it means 'pushing upward' or 'effort.'"

"I understand," said Tan.

"The last figure is that of the youngest daughter (☱). Its name is Tui (dway), and its symbol is a marsh or a reservoir of water or a lake. It is not these things, but it is like these things. It has a feeling attached to it, that of joyousness." Fu Hsi stopped and looked at Tan quietly, then asked, "Do you understand all that I have said to you?"

Tan said immediately, "Yes, great master, I understand and remember all that you have said. I go over my lessons again and again in my thoughts. I can hear your exact words as clearly when I am not with you as I do now. I draw the kua in my thoughts as I do in the dust. I think about them continually. Before I go to sleep, I see them all, and upon waking, I see them again. I hear your voice telling me of them when I prepare the tea, when I tend the garden, when I cleanse myself, when I gather the firewood. The kua live inside my head and move as though they were alive."

Fu Hsi nodded and smiled. "It is well that you do these things," he said, "for there is much to learn. This is only the beginning, but in all beginnings there lie the seeds that contain the image of the end. A master," he said, looking at Tan with his piercing gaze, "can see the end in the beginning.

These," he said, pointing to the symbols Tan had drawn in the dust, "are the eight great kua. They stand for all the forces that are at work in heaven and on earth. It is through the interaction of these forces that all things in heaven and on earth come into being and act as they do. It is only through the interaction of these forces that events take place and destiny fulfills itself. When the darkness of K'an grows, it is only because the light of Li is receding. When the light of Li grows, it can only do so by overcoming the darkness of K'an.

"When the arousing power of Chén beckons a little tree seed, the seed responds and begins to grow. After the tree has risen high above the ground and we see it growing, Tui causes us to feel joy. In the end, Ken, with its stopping power, halts the progress of the tree, and K'an with its dangerous cold comes and kills the tree."

Tan stared down at the ground a long moment and then said, "In a way that seems sad."

"It would be sad," said Fu Hsi, "if that were the end of the story." Tan looked up expectantly. "Every ending contains a new beginning," said the old sage, and he smiled his lovely, warm smile. "Remember that, my son, every ending contains a new beginning."

CHAPTER TEN
The Void

Fu Hsi and Tan were sitting cross-legged on cushions that Tan had placed on some flat rocks near the little waterfall at the rear of Fu Hsi's house. The sun warmed them while the sounds from the waterfall and the little stream created soft musical sounds. Birds sang in the trees, and the wind made a gentle sound through the pine needles. It was serenely peaceful. Fu Hsi said, "It is time for you to enter into the Void."

"The Void? Where is that?"

"That is what I call the space where everything exists before it is formed. It is as if you had an image in your mind of a figure, and then you carved the figure out of wood. Before the wooden figure emerged, the idea of it was in your thoughts. It is the same with everything that exists; an image of everything exists in the Void before it is created, a perfect image. Do you know what a mold is?"

"Yes. I have a shell into which I pack wet sand. Then I turn the shell upside down and tap it lightly, then I remove the shell. The sand remains formed in the image of the shell. The shell is a mold."

"Exactly."

Tan opened his mouth to ask whether there was a mold for himself, but then he realized that Fu Hsi had just told him that everything had a mold, so he closed his mouth and withheld his question.

Fu Hsi, who seemed to miss nothing, smiled and said, "Yes, you too have a mold."

Tan colored a bit but recovered quickly from his small embarrassment and said, "Revered Master, do the images from which all things come change?"

Fu Hsi smiled. "Are you asking that question because you have seen that everything is always changing?"

This time Tan had to comment, "You always seem to be able to read my thoughts. Yes, that is why I ask."

"That is a good question. The answer is that the image is fully formed, including all of its states of change, from its birth to its seeming death, all at the same time."

"That is a difficult concept for me to hold. Does that mean that All-That-Is thinks?"

"Do you think?"

"Yes."

"Are you part of All-That-Is?"

Tan thought for a moment, then said, "I understand Great Master. Is it that way with everything? If I feel fear or happiness or hatred or love, are those things part of All-That-Is?"

Fu Hsi said nothing, only looked at Tan with a serene countenance.

Tan dipped his head in a little bow and said, "I understand Great Master."

Fu Hsi remained silent, allowing Tan to fully grasp the new thought.

Tan tried to imagine the Void. "When I enter the Void," he asked, "will I be able to see the images of everything that exists?"

"You do not see as you do with your eyes; you become aware of images. It is the work of a lifetime just to become aware of some of the images."

"How shall I begin?"

"You begin by sitting correctly. The position you are in now, with your legs crossed in front of you, the top of each foot resting on the opposite thigh, is correct. It provides you with a strong seat, one that will prevent you from falling over while you are in the Void. Now, touch the tip of each thumb to the tip of the finger alongside it, forming a circle. The other fingers are relaxed, perhaps slightly curled. Now, rest your wrists on your knees, palms facing nearly straight upwards; sit straight, touch the tip of your tongue to the back of the roof of your mouth; do not strain. Everything must be done gently. If you attempt to obtain by force that which can only be obtained by gentleness and calmness, it will lead to unwholesome results. Now, close your eyes and fix your attention on your breathing."

Tan was excited by the prospect of entering the Void, and a little frightened. He closed his eyes, then immediately opened them wide asking, "The Void, is it in me?"

"Inside, outside, it is all the same. Close your eyes and concentrate on your breath."

Tan did as he was told but immediately noticed that he was breathing rapidly. He took several deep breaths to calm himself, then again fixed his attention on his breathing. He could sense his master's eyes upon him. No, that wasn't quite right; he could sense his master's awareness of him, almost as if the great Fu Hsi were inside his head with him. With that insight, Tan felt his fear leave him, and he relaxed.

Fu Hsi said immediately, "Good, my son, very good." Then they sat silently. Tan, concentrating on his breathing, noticed the way his chest rose and fell, felt the air move gently through his nose. Within less than a minute, Tan had lost his concentration on his breathing and found himself thinking of his village. Fu Hsi said in a whisper, "When your thoughts carry you away from concentrating on your breathing, the path to the Void is lost." Tan immediately brought his attention back to his breathing. Fu Hsi said quietly, "Whenever you find that your thoughts have drifted, gently pull your attention back to your breathing." Tan sat up straighter and focused his attention sharply on his breathing. "Gently," said Fu Hsi, "gently." Tan relaxed. Fu Hsi said quietly, "For the rest of your life, you will spend a portion of every day in this manner." Then he fell silent, entered the Void, and in that way they passed the afternoon.

CHAPTER ELEVEN

Fu Hsi's Dream

The next afternoon Fu Hsi and Tan were sitting on the platform that extended over the abyss. Fu Hsi said, "After I worked with the kua for many years and had learned much more about them, I was shown that each of them has a tendency either to rise or fall by the nature of its inherent qualities. Can you tell me in which direction each of the kua move?"

Tan looked thoughtfully out over the abyss, past the mountains to the plain and the river far below. His thoughts, however, were not on the distant plains, but on the images moving in his mind. He saw the figure of Ken (☶), and he said, "Ken, the mountain, ponderous, broad-based, heavy, sinks down." Fu Hsi smiled and lightly slapped the side of his staff with his fingers in applause. Tan glowed inwardly. He liked nothing better than to bask in the admiration of his great master. Conversely, he liked nothing less than to awaken the lightning flash of his master's eyes by appearing foolish or incompetent.

Tan said, "Ch'ien (☰), heaven, light, airy, expansive, rises." Fu Hsi nodded, and Tan continued. "K'un (☷), earth, heavy, cold, sinks. Li (☲), fire, bright, light, rises. K'an (☵), the abyss, water, always flowing down, sinks down. Chên (☳) thunder, the arousing, flies upward."

He stopped and looked at Fu Hsi who nodded with a sparkle in his eyes and said, "Good, my son, good. Continue."

Tan hesitated. "The direction of the last two kua are not clear to me great master. It seems that Sun (☴), wood, which, as a tree grows upward and as the penetrating wind blows over the earth, would tend to rise, and that Tui (☱), as the marsh or the lake, would sink down, much the same as K'an, but as I was sure with the other kua, of these two I am not sure."

"Very good; excellent. I, too, was confused about those two kua for awhile, but as I continued to enter the Void, it became clear to me that Tui rises because of its attribute of joyousness, and Sun sinks because of its attribute of penetration."

"How did you learn that the kua rose or sank?"

"It was shown to me in a dream. Long before I became Emperor of China, I dreamed I was Emperor. In my dream we were fighting a mighty war with people of another land. The war went on and on, it seemed, for many years, and I was greatly wearied. I thought it would never end. I was so tired that I looked up to heaven and asked, 'Will this war never end? I am so tired; will there ever be peace again?' Then I saw emerging from the Huang Ho, (the Yellow River) a dragon horse."

Tan asked excitedly, "Is it true that the dragon horse has teeth like those of a tiger, teeth that can tear a lion to shreds?"

Fu Hsi smiled and replied, "The horse is only a mythical figure, but, yes, the horse I saw in my dream was extremely powerful and his teeth were pointed and sharp. His great muscles rippled under his coat, and when he snorted, flames came from his nostrils. He was pure white except for the markings on his side."

"What did the marks look like?"

Fu Hsi closed his eyes in remembrance. "I watched him run cross the plain, sparks shooting from under his hoofs when they struck the rocky ground, and then he came near me and presented his side so I could clearly see the markings—they were the eight great kua arranged in a circle. As I looked, the kua began to fade and then disappeared, and in their place appeared the kua of K'un

(☷), Earth, and Ch'ien, (☰) Heaven. K'un was over Ch'ien (䷊) and as I watched, the horse rippled his skin, and K'un began to sink downward while Ch'ien began to rise, the two merging.

"As they came together, bright rainbows flowed from the kua and flew up into the sky over the dragon horse, and brilliant light shone down on all the land. The fighting stopped, and the soldiers of both sides threw down their weapons and came together and embraced; there was peace. Heaven and Earth had merged. Flowers appeared on the fields, and birds sang. My tiredness left me, and I was wonderfully refreshed. There was great rejoicing, truly, a time of Heaven on Earth.

"As I continued to watch, the kua on the side of the dragon horse separated, became K'un over Ch'ien again, and then, with each ripple of the horse's skin, the lines changed; broken lines became whole, and whole lines became broken, each time forming a different six-line kua. I watched for a long time as the lines formed and reformed, creating many combinations."

Tan exclaimed, "You were not only shown that the kua rise or fall, but that they can be combined, and that the broken and unbroken lines transform one into the other."

Fu Hsi nodded and sighed deeply. He said, "That is correct. It was a great moment for me and for all people on earth. In that dream I was shown that all situations in Heaven and on Earth can be known. I realized that by placing each of the eight three-line kua over itself and also over the other seven, they would produce a total of sixty-four kua. Each one of the kua, by changing one or more of its lines, can become any one of the other sixty-three kua. Each of the sixty-four kua represents a condition or situation, and within each condition or situation there exist the six stages of change, each stage represented by one of the six lines of the kua. Because any one of the kua can change into any one of the other kua, there are a total of 4,096 different possibilities. [64 × 64] Many years were to pass before I was able to perceive the full meaning of the sixty-four kua." Fu Hsi fell silent, and his face, turned upward toward the sky, was a mask of radiant, fragile beauty.

Tan looked at his master and thought, "How like a God he is."

Fu Hsi spoke without opening his eyes. "The sixty-four kua are nothing less than a tiny model of All-That-Is, a perfect representation, including all states of change. The sixty-four kua contain the past, the present, and the future." Fu Hsi opened his eyes and looked at Tan, and said in a whisper, "The past, the present, and the future are one."

Tan's eyes opened wide, and his jaw fell in astonishment. Fu Hsi continued. "Change makes the past, present, and future seem different; however, all change takes place within an ever-present 'now.' The past, present, and future seem different to us because we perceive with our bodies, our senses, but we must not be deceived by what our bodies and our senses tell us." He reached over and gently raised Tan's jaw saying, "I have seen beyond this existence, to the oneness of all."

The concept was too much for Tan. He sat there for many minutes, mesmerized. Finally, he shook himself and came back to the moment.

Fu Hsi continued. "It seems to us as if there is an endless past that stretches behind us and an endless future that stretches ahead, while we exist on the tiny hairline of time we call 'now,' a hairline that separates the future from the past. Actually, the reverse is true; all there is, and was, and ever will be, is an eternal, ever-present 'now,' within which change takes place." Tan was still trying vainly to grasp the enormity of the new concept when his teacher stood up and said, "Within this particular moment of now, will the everlasting Tan prepare tea for us?"

Tan leaped to his feet and darted away, his head whirling with images of dragon horses with teeth like those of a tiger and symbols that magically transformed themselves one into another.

CHAPTER TWELVE

The Fifth Teaching

Fu Hsi and Tan were sitting on the logs in the garden, Tan on the lower log and Fu Hsi on the upper. Fu Hsi was holding his ebony staff with both hands, the tip of it firmly planted in the ground. Tan looked at Fu Hsi with concern. His master seemed tired that day. He had been quiet for about ten minutes. Tan asked timidly, "Is all well with you Great Master?"

Fu Hsi said slowly, "With every falling leaf, the oak tree grows older. Soon it will be time for me to leave this body. As the time grows nearer, I sometimes feel tired."

Tan was alarmed. "Great Master! What are you saying? Are you ill?"

Fu Hsi shook his head slowly. "No, my son, I am not ill, just old, and sometimes tired. I am nearly ready to depart this earth. My final task is to start the great wisdom on its long journey through the millennia. I will impart it to you, and you will impart it to the next one chosen, and he will pass it on in his turn to a future generation, and it shall not perish from the land. Emperors and Kings will come and go, great winters and severe droughts will occur, civilizations will rise and fall, the people of the earth will see many great wonders and amazing changes, great religions will spring up bringing new teachings and then will pass away, but the wisdom I pass along to you shall persist."

Tears sprang to Tan's eyes. Surely, he had never expected to lose his teacher so soon after finding him. He blurted out, "Great Master, you cannot go! I—I have just found you."

Fu Hsi looked at Tan, and the lightning came into his eyes as he stamped his staff on the ground. "What's this? Tears? Have you not heard anything I have said? Did you not hear me say that every ending has a new beginning? Am I not included in that?"

Tan hung his head and said quietly, "I heard you Revered Master, but I have not your great wisdom and understanding, and all I can think of is that you will be gone, and, even though it be to a new beginning, I will miss you terribly."

The lightning faded from Fu Hsi's eyes, and he nodded. "I understand, my son. But it will be all right; you will be all right—I have seen it."

They sat quietly for awhile, the bees creating a low hum as they busied themselves among the blossoms of Fu Hsi's garden. At last, Fu Hsi spoke. "I am going to tell you something of the sixty-four kua, and then you will go back to the village for the winter. In the spring you shall come again. Upon your return, I will teach you all about the sixty-four kua and the way to investigate the past, present, and future with the help of yarrow stalks."

"How will I know when to return?" asked Tan.

"Do not concern yourself over that; one morning, at the beginning of spring, you will awaken and know the time for your return has come. During that spring, summer, and fall I will teach you all you need to know; then it will be time for you to depart, and also for me to depart."

Tan's grief was like a hot pain within his breast, but he withheld any outward sign of it, except for a trembling lower lip, and said, "But Great Master, what will you do during the winter? Who will care for you? Why may I not remain here with you?"

"Your concern does you credit, my son. But you must return to your village for the winter. I will remain here and compose the great poem which you will memorize; for that I need solitude. Do not worry about me. I have been through many winters. Now we must begin our lesson for today."

Tan was not at all sure that everything was going to be all right, or that he would wake up one day with the sure knowledge that he was to return to his master, but he reminded himself that he had resolved to believe without question everything his great master told him. He closed his eyes and concentrated on his breathing to calm himself; Fu Hsi waited. After a few minutes, Tan opened his eyes, settled himself on the log, and gave Fu Hsi his complete attention as the old sage began to speak.

"Each of the eight great kua combines with itself and with the other seven to produce sixty-four kua of six lines each. Each six-line kua represents a condition or situation in heaven or on earth; and within each condition or situation are six stages of change, each stage represented by a line. In the sixty-four kua of six lines each, there are three hundred eighty-four stages of change, each stage represented by a line. Taken all together, the sixty-four kua represent a movement, a cycle, from its beginning to its end, such as the four seasons of the year, or a full day, or from the beginning of a project to its end. If we arranged the sixty-four kua in a circle, each six-line kua would represent one step of the circle. The first line at the bottom of each six-line kua represents the onset of a condition, such as the condition of 'Holding Back In The Face Of Danger' (䷄). The condition progresses through its six stages, beginning with the first line, which represents the start of the waiting when danger has not yet appeared, and ends with the top line which indicates that the waiting is over because the danger has come; then the next condition begins."

"What is the next condition?" asked Tan.

"It depends on the action you took during the condition of 'Waiting In The Face Of Danger.' If you were wise and took the correct steps, you could have caused the onset of the condition of 'Peaceful Prosperity And Harmony, Heaven On Earth' (䷊). If you were unwise and engaged in foolish action, you could have caused the onset of the condition of 'Persecution' (䷣) or another of the conditions that are dangerous and unpleasant. According to the action you take in any situation or condition, any other condition or situation symbolized by the other sixty-three kua can be initiated."

Tan thought for a moment and then his eyes opened wide and he looked at Fu Hsi in astonishment. Fu Hsi nodded and smiled. Tan said, "That means that by choosing our actions we can bring about any condition we desire."

Fu Hsi lightly slapped his staff in applause. "Very good, my son, very good. There is more to it than that, but, generally speaking, by acting in a certain manner, you can cause the onset of any condition that you desire."

"Is that not the most valuable piece of information in the world?"

Fu Hsi smiled again and nodded. "It is one of the most valuable pieces—there are others."

"Is there an order of the sixty-four kua that exists in the Void? No, wait, I don't mean that. You have told me that everything exists in the Void and that means that the order exists there as well. What I mean is—well, what do I mean?"

"I know what you want to know, and it is a good question. It is true that everything exists in the Void, including all orders, but what you really want to know is if an 'original' order exists. Yes, I believe that there is an order that I call the 'natural' order. I call it the natural order because it follows the path ordained by natural law. I will draw the natural order for you here in the dust."

As Fu Hsi slowly drew the sixty four symbols, Tan thought to himself that what Fu Hsi was saying was so complex and so far removed from Tan's former world that his impulse was to say, "Wait. This is too much for me. I cannot grasp all this." At the same time, however, he understood exactly what Fu Hsi was saying, and it was all very clear to him.

Fu Hsi completed drawing the sixty-four kua. They were arranged in a square eight columns across and eight columns down:

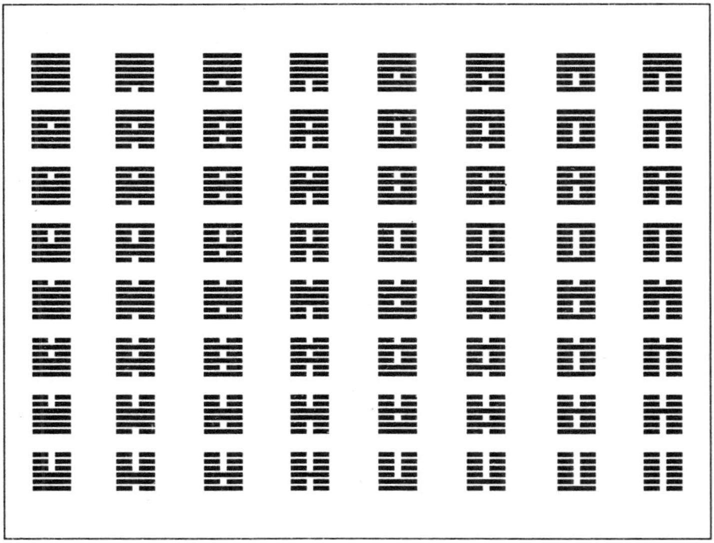

Tan studied the square for a long time. He saw that there was a sequence that repeated itself. Then he closed his eyes and envisioned the sixty-four kua. As he beheld the figures, the bottom line of the first figure began to pulsate; then the pulsation stopped, and the line above it began to pulsate; then it stopped and the third line began. Each in its turn, with no change in rhythm, the lines pulsated and stopped, the movement flowing from the bottom of one six line kua to its top, beginning anew at the bottom of the next six line kua, and so continued until the end was reached and the pulsation began anew at the beginning. Tan opened his eyes and looked at Fu Hsi who sat watching him, smiling.

Fu Hsi said, "Two thousand years from now, another sage will appear on earth who will change the order of the kua. He and his son will bring greater understanding of the kua to the land."

"How can you know this Great Master?"

"With the help of the yarrow stalks one can know all things."

Tan fell silent for awhile, then asked, "Great Master, after we die, do we ever come back to the earth"?

Fu Hsi looked off into the distance, his hands clasped around his shining black staff, then he looked at Tan with a twinkle in his eye and asked, "Are we here now?"

"Yes, most assuredly."

"Well then, it seems as if we know how to get here. We may have forgotten how we came to earth this time, but we are here. What we've done once, we can do again."

"I would like to come back again when you are here, Great Master."

Fu Hsi, smiled and said, "I believe that the father and son I told you about, the ones who will change the order of the kua two thousand years from now, will be you and me—the son's name is Tan—I have seen it."

Tan was excited. "Will we know it is us?"

"That I do not know." Fu Hsi spoke slowly. "It seems that since previous lifetimes are hidden from us now, we will most likely not know about past lifetimes in the future."

Fu Hsi rose and walked to the little waterfall and sat down. Tan sat facing him. "Sometimes though," he said, "a soul is given the power to know the past and the future, as it was given to me in this lifetime. Then those things can be known."

"In that lifetime, two thousand years from now, will we know about this lifetime?"

Fu Hsi's eyes twinkled with mirth again as he replied, "I think you had better wait and ask me then. Now, I have a question for you: have you understood all that I have said?"

Tan did not hesitate even a moment, but said, "Yes,

Great Master. Each of the eight three-line kua combines with itself and the other seven, one at a time, to form the sixty-four six-line kua. Each of the six-line kua represents a condition or situation. Within each of the sixty-four kua there are six lines, each line representative of a stage of the condition or situation represented by the kua. Movement within the kua is from the bottom line to the top line, and from there, the movement passes on to the next six-line figure which is representative of another condition or situation which also goes through its six stages of change, the movement continuing until all sixty-four kua have, in their turn, come and gone." He glanced at Fu Hsi, who nodded.

"Taken as a whole, the sixty-four kua represent a complete cycle, or movement, consisting of sixty-four parts. If we placed the sixty-four kua in a circle, each one would represent a segment of the circle. When movement has progressed completely around the circle in sixty-four steps, the beginning is reached again." Tan paused, then said, "And we come back to earth, living many lifetimes."

In the time that Tan had been with Fu Hsi, he had grown ever more sensitive to the great sage. There were times when Tan thought he knew what his master was thinking. Several times when the feeling was particularly strong he had almost voiced his thoughts but had held his speech for fear of appearing too forward. Now, however, he sensed that his master was about to ask him to prepare tea, and so strong was the sensation. that he arose, bowed, and said, a little tremulously, "My great master desires that I prepare tea?" Fu Hsi's countenance reflected his pleasure of Tan's perception, and he lightly slapped his staff again and nodded. Tan bowed and hurried off, elation welling up within him.

The next day, Fu Hsi sent Tan on his way back to the village with sufficient supplies for the journey, a few messages for the villagers, and strong words of caution to Tan about maintaining modesty. Tan was still uneasy about leaving his master alone to face the cruel winter he knew was coming and even more uneasy about knowing when to return, but he bravely took his leave without another word. He merely bowed low, turned, and left. Fu Hsi watched Tan until he was out of sight, then he turned and made his way slowly back to the garden where he seated himself, his face raised toward the sun, and entered the Void.

CHAPTER THIRTEEN

The Homecoming

In the early evening of his ninth day of walking, Tan met a messenger who was returning to the village from another direction. After they exchanged greetings, the messenger hurried away with a new message to deliver, and Tan prepared to stop for the evening.

Tan knew that his return to the village would be difficult. The wayward, irresponsible youth, the young man of whom the elder had said, "I'd rather send a cow," the last choice in the village, was returning home as "the chosen one."

That evening, as he sat before his small fire eating rice and vegetables from Fu Hsi's garden, he remembered his teacher's final words of caution as he was leaving: "Modesty, my son, modesty." Tan resolved that no matter what happened, he would not discredit his great master.

He was up before dawn, and after cleansing himself at the nearby stream and entering into the Void for two hours, he munched a few handfuls of rice from his previous night's dinner and was back on the path home. As he walked, he silently chanted one word for each step: modesty . . . modesty . . . modesty.

Even with Fu Hsi's caution and his own preparation, Tan was not prepared for the scene that greeted him early that evening when he was still half a mile from home; the path, which had broadened, was lined on either side by the people of his village. Nearly two thousand people had turned out to welcome him. Only the infirm and the very elderly were not there, but even those had been moved out to the street in the village so they could see the returning hero and help in welcoming him home.

As he approached, the villagers began cheering and chanting his name: "Tan! Tan! Tan!" Small children ran to him carrying flowers which they thrust into his arms; then they held onto his shirt and trousers, and as they walked along together, the children chanted in their high piping voices, "Tan, Tan, Tan."

Tan felt his face flush with embarrassment. He didn't know what to do. He was overwhelmed by the display of acclaim. He bowed his head and walked steadily on, chanting over and over in his mind, "Modesty, modesty, modesty."

As they reached the village, he was greeted by the elders along with Tan's mother and father. Tan bowed to his parents and then to the elders. There were tears in his mother's eyes and a broad smile on his father's face. To the chief elder he said, "I bring you greetings from our revered master, Fu Hsi. He thanks you for the gifts you have sent to him. He said I should say to you that the first snows will come twenty-one days before the winter solstice."

The chief elder bowed to him and said, "We are indebted to the great Fu Hsi whose wisdom knows no bounds—and we are indebted to you for the warning you gave to us after the great harvest which set into motion all that has now come to pass. I know you are eager to spend time with your parents, but the whole village has turned out to welcome you. We have arranged a feast in your honor which is now about to begin. Please delay the time to be with your parents to allow us to show our appreciation for the great gift of the warning you brought to us and also for the honor you have brought to our village by being chosen as Fu Hsi's disciple."

Tan bowed to the chief elder and said, "All credit goes to my parents and to my teacher, the great Fu Hsi. Whatever honors I receive, I receive on their behalf."

The elder raised his eyebrows in appreciation at this display of modesty and turned to the other elders and nodded as if to say, "See what a great treasure we have in this young man? How could we have been so blind?" Then he turned and led the way to the center of the village where a huge fire burned.

Slabs of meat were roasting, and many long tables had been laid with fresh fruits, vegetables, and flowers. People were playing musical instruments and children danced about. The platform reserved for the elders had been decorated with fall leaves and flowers.

The chief elder mounted to the platform and the other elders filed up after him, each taking his assigned seat to either side of the chief elder. Tan stood directly below him. The chief elder waited for quiet and then spoke. "My fellow villagers, it is with great honor that we receive into our midst once again, our fellow villager, Tan." There was great cheering and hand clapping that continued for some time. Tan's face flushed with embarrassment. He looked down at the ground and thought of Fu Hsi. How would his great master have acted? He turned, faced the villagers and put his hands high in the air, then, with his arms fully extended, he bowed low to the people. A great roar went up from the crowd at the honor he thus bestowed upon them. Drums were beaten, and musical instruments sounded as the people cheered.

The chief elder finally restored quiet and continued. "Our most revered and honored guardian, Fu Hsi, sent word through his disciple, Tan, that the first snows will begin twenty-one days before the winter solstice. That means that the snow will come in three days." There were murmurs from the crowd. How could Fu Hsi know the exact day the snow would begin? The elder continued. "Because of this young man," he indicated Tan standing in front of the platform, "we were warned in time and we are all well prepared." Another round of cheering ensued.

The elder restored quiet and said, "Will the young man who has brought so much honor to our village come up onto the stage and say a few words?" He beckoned to Tan to move onto the stage where a special chair had been placed.

When he saw the place of honor that was reserved for him, Tan inwardly shrank, thinking, "How shall I maintain my modesty in the face of this honor?" Surely, he thought, Fu Hsi could not have foreseen this. But no sooner had the thought entered his mind than he realized that Fu Hsi had seen all this very clearly and had prepared him for it as well as he could with his cautioning. So he bowed to the elders and mounted the steps to the platform, his heart beating wildly. The villagers cheered and crowded as near to the platform as they could.

Tan waited until the crowd quieted and the only sound was the crackle of the fire. The place for the platform had been selected because it was a natural amphitheater, surrounded on three sides by hills. Words spoken in a normal tone of voice could be heard by the last person in the crowd as easily as the first. Tan began. "I bring you greetings from our revered master, Fu Hsi. I thank you in his behalf for the honor you show to his disciple. I thank you for the honor you show to my parents. Please think of me as a messenger, an empty vessel that Fu Hsi is filling with his great wisdom so that I will be able to give it to you, and you will be able to give it to your children, and they to theirs, and Fu Hsi's wisdom shall not perish from the world."

There were nods from the crowd and a low buzz as they commented to each other concerning the humble manner in which Tan accepted his honor. Surely it was fitting that he was the chosen one.

Tan continued. "I know you want to hear about the Great Fu Hsi, and so I shall now do my best to tell you what I know. Of all the stories you have heard of the great sage ruler, even though they were magnified a hundred times, none can do him the honor he deserves. Of all people, he is the most worthy, the most honorable, the wisest. The wisdom of the world flows through him like a sparkling brook through the forest. When he speaks, time seems to cease."

Tan paused and someone spoke from the middle of the crowd. "What is it like to be with him?"

Tan said, "When he frowns, I shudder with an inward fear that I have displeased him. His lightning glance is able to freeze my very bones. When he smiles, it is as if the sun has come out from behind a cloud. When he speaks, he opens the mysteries of the world as we open pods to disclose the peas hidden within." There was another buzz of comments from the crowd and nods of assent. Tan said, "He moves with complete grace. He is old, very old, and he is cloaked with great dignity and virtue; it seems to me that he is as pure as new fallen snow."

"Is it true that at night he turns himself into a dragon and flies over the kingdom seeking out evil-doers?"

"He does not need to transform himself into a dragon," said Tan; "he *is* a dragon. Neither does he have to fly over the kingdom to know what is happening. He knows the past, the present, and the future; he knows of things near at hand and far away. Of what need would he have to go flying about at night as a dragon to seek out evil-doers? As for me, he sees into the heart of my very being. He knows what I am thinking."

Steam issued from mouths and nostrils in the cold night air. Tan paused, thinking about what Fu Hsi had said regarding his imminent departure from his earthly form. A wave of sadness passed through him, but he said nothing of that and continued, "There is an aura of light that hovers about him. I cannot see the light if I look at it directly, but if I look slightly away, off to the side, I can see it. I know it is not my imagination; there truly is a white light that emanates from him. My most honored master never speaks a careless word, nor makes a careless action, nor does anything escape him.

"One day when I threw a cup of water onto the ground in a spot barren of vegetation, he scolded me for wasting the water. He said I should have given the gift of the water to a plant." That caused a hum of response to arise, and Tan waited until there was quiet.

He looked out over the crowd and said, "There is nothing I can say to you that would do that most venerable man justice. To use all the words that exist fall as short of the mark as if I were to try to remove the great mountain with a pointed stick. One thing I can tell you, and it is the most important thing of all." The crowd quieted until only the fire could be heard, and into that silence Tan said, "He loves all of you and cares for all of you as if you were his very own children."

A murmur of appreciation went through the crowd. Tan bowed to them and stepped down from the platform. He was immediately surrounded by a group of villagers who wanted to ask questions. Soon the feast began, and there was music and dancing. Later, a play was performed. It told the story of a young man, a ne'er-do-well, who was chosen by the great Fu Hsi to become his disciple. Much to Tan's relief and pleasure, it was a comedy, and much fun was made of the young man who could not get his lessons right and was forever making mistakes.

Three days later, the first fierce snowstorm of winter began as predicted and did not cease for ten days. So long and hard did it snow that the village was covered, and people had to make tunnels to move about. Temperatures dropped below freezing. Tan spent most of his time in the small room that had been built for him at the back of his parents' home. There, he entered the Void. Many hours each day he sat in the lotus position, his concentration turned inward. He knew that Fu Hsi's spirit was hovering about. He could sense it, and he knew that his great master was watching over him. Deep inside, Tan still carried the fear that he would not know the right time to return to his master. Even though he knew he shouldn't be concerned, he was.

All during the long and severe winter, Tan studied the kua. He took them with him into the Void, or, rather, in the Void he found them. He saw the eight kua of three lines each form and merge with each other, creating the sixty-four great kua. He began to perceive the meanings of the sixty-four kua, and one day he realized that Fu Hsi was instructing him. Then he knew that he need not have any fear of missing the time to return. He knew he would be summoned, and that he would hear the summons as clearly as if Fu Hsi was standing in the room with him. Later, when he was on his way back to Fu Hsi, he would think back on that moment of realization and smile.

A part of each day was set aside to instruct the eight young men who had been chosen as potential disciples to Fu Hsi. Tan taught them what he had learned, and they were exceedingly grateful that Tan had chosen to pass his knowledge along to them to give to the rest of the villagers, thereby restoring their honor.

In this manner the severe winter passed. Early in the spring, when the last snows had melted from the lower valleys, Tan awoke one morning with the vision of Fu Hsi standing before him, smiling and beckoning to him. At first Tan did not know whether he was dreaming or awake, but when he shook his head and rubbed his eyes and blinked several more times and the vision persisted, he knew it was real. Fu Hsi smiled and beckoned again, and the vision faded. Tan laughed with sheer joy, leaped from his bed, and began to pack his few possessions for the return journey. He bade his parents farewell, promising to take care of himself, visited the elders to say goodbye, gave final instructions to the eight young men he was teaching, and was soon on his way from the village. Word had spread quickly that Tan was returning to Fu Hsi, and the many of the people turned out to see him off. Children ran alongside him, holding on to his pants or shirt, and the villagers walked along with them. At the outskirts of the village, he turned, put his hands together in front of his face as though he were praying, bowed to everyone, and with a lightness of heart and a gladness of spirit, turned his footsteps toward the high mountains. The villagers looked after him until he entered the forest half a mile away where he turned and waved a final farewell to them.

CHAPTER FOURTEEN

The Sixty-Four Great Kua

When Tan arrived at Fu Hsi's house he found him in the garden. Alongside the sage on a flat-topped rock was a steaming pot of tea, a pot of freshly made rice, two cups, two bowls, and two pairs of chopsticks. Tan was so glad to see his great master that tears came to his eyes as he dropped to his knees and lowered his head until his forehead touched the earth. Fu Hsi tapped him on the shoulder and simply indicated that Tan was to take his usual seat on the log. They drank their tea and ate their rice in silence. Tan glanced often at his master, only to see him gazing at the flowers of his garden as if Tan had not been away the whole long winter.

At first glance, Fu Hsi looked much the same as when Tan left for his village in the fall. However, after Tan had cautiously observed the old sage for awhile, he noticed that he was thinner, and the skin on his hands was a bit more like old parchment, the blue veins showing through. He seemed somehow more delicate, as if the brutal winter had further refined him in some way. Also, his eyes were different. Last year when he had looked at Tan there was a bright, piercing intensity in his eyes that had held Tan as if he were a butterfly stuck with a thorn onto a mat. Now, when Fu Hsi glanced at Tan, that same fiery intensity was there, but trebled. Tan felt as though Fu Hsi now held the power of the sun in his eyes, and, if he chose, he could melt Tan as the sun melts snow. Tan knew that whatever had happened to Fu Hsi while he was away, the great sage now was imbued with a power far beyond anything Tan could comprehend.

Tan cleared away the cups, bowls, teapot, and chopsticks and resumed his seat.

Fu Hsi turned to him and the weight of his gaze cleared all thoughts from Tan's mind, leaving it wonderfully clear and open. "The first of the sixty-four great kua is Ch'ien (䷀)." He drew the figure in the dust with the tip of his staff. "It is made by doubling the three-line kua also called Ch'ien. It is the father figure; its force is the creative. As such, it represents the condition of creating. Do you know what the six lines of Ch'ien represent?"

"Yes, Great Master. They represent the six stages of bringing anything into being."

Fu Hsi smiled. "I see you have spent your time well this winter."

"Of course, Great Master, you would know that because you were with me." He tapped his head, "Here, inside."

Fu Hsi reached over and touched Tan's heart, "There, too." Tan inclined his head in acknowledgment. Fu Hsi said, "This spring and summer, I am going to teach you, in order, the sixty-four kua, what situation or condition each represents, and what each of the lines means. You will also learn to use the fifty yarrow stalks that will enable you to know all things. In the fall, after you have learned those things, I will teach you the great poem that you will carry with you back into the world."

The way Fu Hsi said "back into the world" made Tan realize that here, on that mountain with the great sage, he actually had stepped out of the world in some way and was living a rare semi-worldly experience. His thoughts turned to the fall of the year after his studies would be completed, and his heart fluttered and a sick feeling entered his abdomen and chest as he realized his teacher would be leaving him.

Fu Hsi stamped the ground with his staff and his eyes flared a bit. Tan collected his thoughts and sat up straight.

"To begin," said the sage, "close your eyes and enter the Void. Do not try to remember anything that I say; remain empty and I will fill you. As I say each of the kua, the six-line image of the kua will appear in your mind. I will then tell you what the kua means and what each of its six lines means."

Tan took a deep breath and slowly exhaled, concentrating on his breathing. He quieted his thoughts; he became still, and in the stillness, he heard his master's voice.*

All that spring and summer, the days flowed one into another as Tan absorbed his lessons. Each day Tan effortlessly awoke an hour before dawn, completely alert, his mind refreshed. As he prepared tea, the six-line figures began to move through his mind, along with their names and meanings. He would bring tea to Fu Hsi who was always sitting on a cushion in the room where Tan had first seen him. They would drink their tea in silence, but such a silence as Tan had never experienced. Al-

* For a complete list of the sixty-four kua, the condition or situation that each one represents, the meaning of each of the 384 lines, and the method of using the yarrow stalks to consult the I Ching, the reader is referred to the book, *The I Ching: The Book of Answers*, interpreted by Wu Wei and available in most bookstores.

though there was no sound but the wind in the trees, the trickling stream, and the occasional bug or animal, the air was alive as if with a physical presence. It seemed as if the intelligence of All-That-Is was in the room, a presence so powerful that Tan felt he could almost reach out and touch it.

After tea, they would enter the Void until the sun was up, then they would go into the garden or elsewhere and begin lessons for the day. After their noon meal, Tan would work with the yarrow stalks. The exercise was a great delight for him, and it never ceased to fill him with wonder that his questions were answered perfectly and with the greatest wisdom.

One day in mid-summer, while Tan was sitting manipulating the yarrow stalks under the watchful eye of Fu Hsi, he stopped and looked up at Fu Hsi and asked, "Since I can ask questions at any time, and since I always receive divinely inspired answers, does that mean I am constantly in the presence of God?"

Fu Hsi smiled. "Yes, and better."

"Better?"

"Do you recall a time last year when I told you that I believed that everything that exists is made from the substance of God?"

"Yes."

"Do you believe that?"

"Yes."

"In that case, are you God?"

"Yes. So—it is like my being in the presence of me?"

"Yes, and more."

"I feel a presence outside myself."

"That is the 'more.' All of you is God, but you are not all of God. A drop of water is all water, but it is not all of the water. The outside presence you detect is the portion of God that is outside of yourself."

Tan nodded his head, wonderingly. He opened his mouth as if to speak, but then said nothing.

Fu Hsi smiled gently and responded to Tan's unspoken statement. "That is correct, my son, you are eternal, as God is eternal. Let me clarify something I said to you last summer. It is not really that every ending has a new beginning, for there are no actual endings or beginnings. Everything simply continues in an endless process of change, one form flowing into another. What we perceive as endings and beginnings are the endings and beginnings of the different forms as they flow into each other."

Tan was silent for many long minutes absorbing what he had heard, and when he looked up, Fu Hsi was sleeping.

CHAPTER FIFTEEN

The Final Chapter

The leaves began to change colors and the days grew shorter as Fu Hsi taught Tan the long poem of the sixty-four kua with their three hundred eighty-four lines. Each line had a particular meaning and specific guidance. As Tan absorbed the material, he grew ever more apprehensive over the prospect of losing his great master whom he had come to love with his whole being. The thought of a world without Fu Hsi was, for him, a world without sunshine.

There finally came a day when Fu Hsi was finished. He let Tan rest a moment and then asked him to recite the entire poem. Tan did as he was asked, but with a sinking heart. One hour became two, and two became three as Tan effortlessly spoke the words taught to him by Fu Hsi. As he neared the end of the poem, tears came to his eyes, and his voice faltered. Fu Hsi's eyes flared and he stamped his staff on the ground. "You must be brave," he exclaimed. "It is only because you are using your imagination to envision a sad ending to this most wonderful time we have had together that you are feeling bad." It was the first time that Fu Hsi had indicated that it had also been a wonderful time for him. "There are great moments that await you in the outside world. You will travel the length and breadth of China, and as you travel you will spread the teaching so that men everywhere will be able to be divinely guided. You will be as highly regarded as the emperor himself."

Tan nodded, wiped his eyes with the back of his hand, and continued to the end of the poem. When he finished, Fu Hsi patted him on the head and said, "Well done, my son. That was perfect." He paused and looked thoughtfully down at the ground, then off into the sky. He said in a contemplative manner, "To the man of true understanding, it makes no difference whether death comes early or late. He cultivates himself and uses his time productively.

"His sense of the transitory nature of life does not impel him to uninhibited revelry to enjoy life while it lasts, nor to yield to melancholy and sadness, thereby spoiling the time remaining to him. Secure in the knowledge that all is one, he experiences himself as a part of All-That-

Is. Knowing that time is only an illusion, he feels no break with time, and therefore has no fear of the moment of death, which is only a point of transition, such as walking through a doorway from one room into another, and no more remarkable than any other moment."

Tan drew in a deep breath and closed his eyes. "I thank you for your wonderful words of wisdom, Great Master. Truly, in the time I have been here, you have opened the doors of my perception, and I am ten thousand times the person I was when I first came here. You have raised me from the level of ignorance and obscurity to the highest plains of knowledge and honor." He opened his eyes and looked at Fu Hsi, put his hands together, and bowed his head, paying tribute to the grand old man. "It is you who perceived all the truths that form the basis of my knowledge. It is you who discovered a way of communicating with All-That-Is. It is you who formulated the answers to every question in heaven and on earth. It is you who opened the path to wisdom and divine guidance for all mankind, and it is you who are the leader.

"I am but your messenger, and as I carry your message forward, I shall link it forever to your name, my Honorable Master, and I shall do everything as well as I can so that I will bring credit and honor to my beloved teacher." He paused, then said in a strained voice, full of emotion, "But oh, master, it is so difficult for me to think of a world in which I will not be able to see you and talk to you, to wake, knowing I will have tea with you and learn from you."

Fu Hsi nodded his head and said, "It is only at the time of parting that the real depths of our love is revealed to us." After a pause he said, "But our time of parting is not yet. Come, I will ask you questions to see whether you have understood all that I have told you since your first arrival." The old man stood and, with the aid of his staff, slowly walked along the path that led to his house from the valley floor, asking questions of Tan.

For the next month and a half, Fu Hsi asked questions that plumbed the depths of Tan's knowledge. Tan responded well, and when his answers fell short, Fu Hsi patiently told him of the great truths of life. He told him about:

human nature

the ways of kings and peasants,

love and hatred, and the way that hate binds a person to the hated object, the laws of nature, rightness and justice,

gain and loss, opportunity and opposition,

good and evil, passion and reason,

the way of the superior person and the way of the inferior person,

salvage and waste, social customs and graces,

yielding and forcing, prosperity and decline,

forgiveness and hard heartedness,

peace and conflict, safety and danger,

the humble and the arrogant and the way they are dealt with by All-That-Is,

forthrightness and deception,

natural action and affected action,

boasting and its effects, good and bad habits,

deliberate action and capriciousness,

strength and weakness, flexibility and rigidity,

goals and aimlessness, hope and fear,

patience and haste, advance and retreat,

gentleness and aggressiveness,

balance and imbalance,
income and expenditures,
simplicity and pretentiousness,
compromise and steadfastness,
loftiness and baseness, leaders and followers,
the spiritual and the physical,
success and failure, fame and obscurity,
rest and movement, meditation and activity,
good fortune and misfortune,
eternity and transitoriness,
meetings and partings, joy and pleasure,
generosity and selfishness,
words and deeds, heaven and earth,
happiness and sadness, reverence and irreverence,
ruling and serving, planting and harvesting,
eating and drinking, moderation and excess,
caution and foolhardiness, and
beginnings and endings.

By the time Fu Hsi finished, the leaves were gone from the trees, and he was walking very slowly, leaning heavily on his staff. It seemed to Tan as if the old man's energy was being concentrated in his mind, that, as he allowed his body to run down, his mind became ever more powerful.

During the past spring, summer, and fall, Tan, in contrast, had grown taller and had filled out physically. He radiated good health and energy. He felt as if he could run all the way to his village and back. In his vitality, he wanted to help his teacher but refrained for fear he might offend the great sage.

The day after Fu Hsi concluded his teaching, Tan awoke and knew the time he had been dreading was at hand. He prepared tea and, as usual, found his master sitting on a cushion in the room where he had first seen him. "How fitting," thought Tan. As always, they drank their tea in silence, then entered into the void. After an hour, Fu Hsi stirred himself and walked into his garden and seated himself on the log where he and Tan had spent so many hours. Tan sat below him on the other log. Fu Hsi said, "I will be leaving you now, my son. After I am gone, please carry my body into the house and place it on my sleeping mat. Then set the house afire. Watch while it burns, and then leave immediately to carry the message and the wisdom to my people—our people."

Tan inclined his head and said, "It shall be as you have said, my master."

Fu Hsi held out his staff to Tan. "I want you to have this." Tan took the staff, but Fu Hsi held onto it. His eyes glittered as they looked into Tan's. "Good-bye—my son—for now." As Tan watched, Fu Hsi took a deep breath, held it a moment, then exhaled, and was gone.

Even though Tan was prepared, the shock of it drove him to his knees. His whole body vibrated, as if the passing of Fu Hsi had been accompanied by an earthquake. The shining black staff vibrated as if it were alive. The tremor finally ceased, and Tan lifted the old man in his arms, marveling that he felt hardly any weight at all, and carried him inside. He laid Fu Hsi on his sleeping palette, crossed the great sage's arms across his chest, and sat near him. Tan's heart was still beating heavily.

After he had calmed down, he arose and went to his room where he took his personal belongings and put them into a sack along with the tea pot, the cups, the bowls, and the chopsticks he and Fu Hsi had used. Then he went to the garden, took enough vegetables for the journey out of the mountains, and picked some of each of the flowers. He took the flowers to Fu Hsi's room and his tears fell as he laid them on the great sage's chest. Lastly, he placed Fu Hsi's yarrow sticks beside him.

Tan used a flat piece of wood to scoop the coals from his morning fire, and these he placed at the base of the house. In moments, the wood of the house was smoldering, and, in a few moments more, the first flames appeared. Tan walked a little ways from the house and turned to face the flames. He sat in the lotus position but kept his eyes open. Soon, the house sent flames leaping to the sky. It seemed to Tan as if it were not possible for fire to burn so brightly or so intensely. After a few minutes, there was a huge updraft of flame that carried sparks and live embers with it. It soared up into the sky with a great roar as if the spirit of Fu Hsi were spewing forth from the earth into the heavens. Higher than the tallest tree the flame leaped, then that flame was gone even as the last of the house was consumed by the blaze.

Tan watched, transfixed. He blinked his eyes, breathed deeply several times, then stood and picked up his sack. He looked all around at this place where he and the great sage had spent so many magical hours. He silently said farewell to everything: the waterfall; the stream; the logs upon which they had sat; the garden; the trees; the rocks, the great mountain rising in back of the house, the smoldering house site. He put his hands together in front of him, prayer fashion, and bowed very low to it all, silently thanking everything. Then he turned and walked along the path that led to the valley.

When he reached the edge of the clearing, he turned, raised the shining black staff in a powerful salute, and bowed low a final time saying, "Until we meet again, Great Master." Then he turned, and, with fire in his eyes and determination in his heart, set forth with purposeful strides on his long journey as the first messenger.

THE END/THE BEGINNING